SLOWLY HE BROUGHT HER INTO HIS ARMS, GIVING HER EVERY OPPORTUNITY TO STOP HIM . . .

But Francyne wouldn't have pulled back at that moment to save her life. The warmth of his body infused her with euphoric abandon. The clean, fresh scent of him drugged her. One arm came around her waist. Strong fingers caressed the back of her neck, wove themselves into the golden brown mane that flowed down her back. Her eyelids fanned against her cheeks, forming dark, sultry crescents on her tanned face. His head bent over hers and she felt his warm mouth cover her own softly parted lips in a gentle, slowly deepening kiss . . .

A CANDLELIGHT ECSTASY ROMANCE ®

RIVER ENCHANTMENT

Emma Bennett

A CANDLELIGHT ECSTASY ROMANCE ®

Published by
Dell Publishing Co., Inc.
1 Dag Hammarskjold Plaza
New York, New York 10017

Dell® TM 681510, Dell Publishing Co., Inc.

Candlelight Ecstasy Romance®, 1,203,540, is a registered
trademark of Dell Publishing Co., Inc., New York, New York.

ISBN: 0-440-17470-8

Printed in the United States of America
First printing—May 1983

To Our Readers:

We have been delighted with your enthusiastic response to Candlelight Ecstasy Romances®, and we thank you for the interest you have shown in this exciting series.

In the upcoming months we will continue to present the distinctive sensuous love stories you have come to expect only from Ecstasy. We look forward to bringing you many more books from your favorite authors and also the very finest work from new authors of contemporary romantic fiction.

As always, we are striving to present the unique, absorbing love stories that you enjoy most—books that are more than ordinary romance. Your suggestions and comments are always welcome. Please write to us at the address below.

Sincerely,

The Editors
Candlelight Romances
1 Dag Hammarskjold Plaza
New York, New York 10017

CHAPTER ONE

"Travel Texas-Style. May I help you?"

Francyne held the phone to her ear while she listened, then she nodded her head, reaching for her note pad and pen.

"Yes, we plan tours for the entire state by bus, van, or car, depending on your budget and on how much time you have."

Her pen raced across the pad as she wrote.

"Certainly! I'll be glad to give you more information. Could you come into the office?" She listened again, writing all the while. "Umhumm, that would be fine," she said, peering at her appointment log. "Will you spell your last name please?" She wrote it down, then spelled it back. "Oh, my name? Francyne LaRue. I'll be expecting you about ten then on Monday morning. Thank you, Mrs. Piermont."

She replaced the receiver, jotted more notes on the sheet of paper, and ripped it off the pad, shoving it into an organizer on her desk. She glanced at her clock and saw that it was nearly twelve. Just enough time to finish this file before lunch, she thought, picking up the yellow file jacket and scanning its contents. After she wrote some instructions on the cover for her secretary, she threw it into her Out basket. No more for this morning. She sighed gratefully. Time to pamper the stomach!

Opening the door on the credenza behind her desk, she picked up her purse and unsnapped it, taking out her cosmetic kit, her brush, and her comb. There was a large mirror on the wall behind the sofa, and she stood before it, brushing her golden brown hair until it hung in silken sheets, caressing her shoulders. Because of her flawless complexion, she wore little makeup. A stroke or two of mascara to her long curling lashes, a little lip gloss, and ready to go, she thought with satisfaction.

"Going to eat?"

Francyne looked around to see her employer, Roberta Ruiz, easing her tiny form into the large velvet chair in front of her desk. She pushed her ringed fingers through the short, thick black hair that framed her face in loose waves. Her eyes were smoky topaz in color, accenting her light brown complexion, and her lips, full and red, were curved into a sad smile.

"Umhumm," Francyne murmured, blotting some of the excess gloss from her lips. It was difficult for her to ignore the sorrow in Roberta's face, but she tried to keep her voice light and impersonal. "I'll have Norma type those files this afternoon. I've checked them, and everything seems to be okay."

"Good," Roberta replied dully, not really interested in the files. She flexed her small shoulders, running her fingers around the expensive gold chain that hung around her neck. "My brother wants me to join him in Mexico."

"Which one?" Francyne asked, moving in the direction of her desk.

"Juan," Roberta replied. "The one who lives on the ranch outside Guadalajara." She shrugged her shoulders in an eloquent, beautiful gesture. "He thinks I need to get away for a while."

Francyne dropped her brush and comb into her purse. "You do," she agreed.

"Do you mind holding the fort down while I'm gone?"

Francyne shook her head, grinning. "I don't mind, but we're certainly going to miss you."

Roberta forced herself to smile, but her large eyes kept their expression of sadness. "Ah, but I'll be having the time of my life," she added.

But even as she spoke the words, both she and Francyne knew it was a lie. Having just come out of a nasty divorce, she wasn't thinking of having fun. She merely wanted to put herself together again and to create a new life.

Francyne saw and understood all this as she watched Roberta's face. "Try to have a good time, Berta," she enjoined gently. "Forget Al. You deserve better than that."

Roberta nodded, blinking back the tears. "I figure I deserve better," she admitted, "but I don't want better. I want him." She held up her hand in front of her face and looked at the ringless fourth finger of her left hand. "So many years," she said faintly. "So much living, so much loving!"

Francyne grinned. "But you've got a lot more living and a lot more loving in store for you."

In spite of herself Roberta chuckled. "When I come back," she declared, standing up, "you won't know me." She put both hands on her hips and swayed across

9

the room. "You won't believe I'm over forty and that my hair color comes out of a bottle." She grinned. "You'll think I'm as young as you are."

Francyne smiled. "You look young now," she replied, truthfully, "and you know you don't have to dye your hair."

Roberta smiled warmly, and Francyne could tell that she was feeling better. "I wanted to let you know that I'm catching an evening flight out." She walked to the door and turned back, one hand on the doorframe. "I'll call sometime during the week to find out how things are going, and I'll let you know when I'm coming home. Do you have Juan's phone number in case you need to reach me?"

Francyne nodded, reaching for her personal phone book. She thumbed through the pages, running her index finger down the column of names. "Yes, I have it, unless it's been changed." She lifted her eyes.

Roberta shook her head. "No, it's the same. Remember," she instructed with her habitual air of authority, "while I'm gone you have the final word."

Francyne grinned. "Okay, chief! Now you have a good time. Maybe Juan can find you a handsome señor or two to occupy your time and to wipe that sadness from your eyes."

Roberta's attempt at a smile came out as more of a grimace. "I'm afraid that's what Juan has in mind. He's of the old school that says a woman isn't complete unless she has a man to wait on." Even though her voice was light and teasing, her next words were underscored with bitterness. "But I'll fool Juan this time. I'm going to find me a man who'll wait on me."

Francyne laughed softly, watching the small figure disappear from the doorway. Then she moved to the mirror, adjusting the collar of her white tailored blouse and retying her navy-and-white scarf around her neck. Satisfied, she stepped back from the mirror and inspected her entire outfit, straightening the seams of her fitted skirt. Pretty good, she thought.

Taking off her blue-rimmed glasses, she pulled her case out of her red straw bag and exchanged them for her large-framed sunglasses. She didn't like having to wear glasses, but she had turned this slight handicap into an advantage. She indulged herself in an assortment of different frames, many colors, sizes, and shapes, whatever suited her mood, fancy, and pocketbook.

The buzz of the intercom broke into her thoughts. Quickly she returned to her desk, lightly touching the button with one hand while she lifted the phone with the other. "Francyne."

"What are you planning to do for lunch?" The voice was brisk and to the point.

"Eat," Francyne shot back, her lips quirking into a grin of sheer devilment, knowing that the obvious answer would irritate Norma.

"Eat where?" Norma demanded curtly; she hated it when Francyne was in one of these moods.

"The usual. Want to go with me?" But she knew the answer before she asked the question. Her secretary, Norma Hollis, made no secret of her feelings about River Walk.

"Oh, Francyne," came the snappy lament, "only tourists eat on the river. Won't you ever get over this obsession you have with that muddy ditch?"

Francyne laughed, seeing the frown of disapproval stamped on Norma's face as plainly as if she were in the same room with her. She could see the tightly drawn features, and she could see Norma raking her hands through her short gray hair. By now, however, Francyne knew that Norma was more bark than bite.

She shoved her glasses up on her nose. "I don't think I'll ever get over it, Norma," she said unashamedly. "Today is too glorious for me to be cooped up inside a department store." She also knew what Norma liked to do during her lunch hour. "I want to enjoy this divine sunshine before the hot weather gets here."

She heard the disappointed sigh. "You know they're having a sale at Joske's?"

Francyne had anticipated this. "Sorry," she replied, "some other time maybe."

"Okay," Norma returned resignedly. "I'm off. See you later."

"Later," Francyne mumbled, dropping the phone in the cradle.

She walked to the large picture window behind her desk, which overlooked the San Antonio River, and stared bemusedly. As many times as she had watched it, and toured it, and walked along its banks she never tired of its simple beauty. This river, which wound its way beneath one of the most colorful, historic cities in the United States, had its own magical world called River Walk, and it had woven its spell around Francyne.

She believed that this small river that flowed in and out of the city wove some kind of magical spell on each person who came near it; this was the gateway to a world that was separated from reality, a world that recognized romance and love. It was a world that Francyne totally enjoyed. She liked its tranquility; she liked the excitement and interest mirrored in the faces of its inhabitants.

She tucked the red straw purse under her arm and went out the back entrance of her building, down the

12

flight of stairs onto the walk. With indolent ease she made her way to one of the many patio restaurants that dotted the River Walk and sat outside, basking in the spring afternoon. She placed her order and sipped her drink while she waited. As usual she people-watched with pleasure, thinking of nothing in particular, enjoying everything in particular.

Her hands rested casually on the table, and her beautiful fingers curved around the base of her glass. Her long, shapely legs were stretched out under the table, crossed at the ankles. She was thoroughly relaxed and happy.

Then she began to feel that eerie sensation that you have when you're being watched. She felt the uncomfortable heat of that penetrating gaze. She wanted to squirm, but she didn't give in to the inclination. With slow deliberation she turned her head, and her hazel eyes, hidden by the darkness of her sunglasses, locked with the most striking brown eyes she'd ever seen.

She was so intrigued by those eyes that she returned his blatant stare, never flinching from its blunt appraisal. Though she could feel the color seeping into her face, she maintained her composure. Without conscious volition, however, she inhaled deeply, amazed at the touching intimacy and the amorous warmth in those eyes.

When the stranger was sure that he had her attention . . . and there had been no doubt in his mind that he would get it sooner or later . . . his lips curved into a smile as warm as his eyes. He raised his glass in salutation, his eyes raking over her entire ensemble—the white blouse, the blue fitted skirt, the blue and white shoes, the red straw bag. He liked what he saw.

"*Hello.*" He mouthed the words silently. "*May I join you?*"

He said no more. He waited to see if she'd respond to his greeting, to see if she was interested. He slowly brought the glass to his lips, looking over the rim, never taking those eyes from her face, never allowing her to break contact.

He did wish, though, that she'd take those glasses off. He wanted to see her eyes. He wanted to know what she was thinking, to look into her inner self. He definitely wanted to see more of her.

Not that he hadn't seen quite a bit, he thought, setting his glass down. He'd been observing her for some time now. In fact, he'd been watching her ever since she walked up. Average height, he guessed. Slender build. He liked that. Wore her clothes well. Nice hips. Nicely rounded all over, in fact. Very good! He particularly appreciated that arrogant tilt of her head, her self-confident gait.

But he hadn't been the only one to notice her arrival, he remembered, a teasing smile hovering on his lips. Her poise and bearing caused everyone to look admiringly at her. She was the sort of person who demanded attention simply because of her presence. Her aura elicited a response—a smile, a nod, a compliment.

Francyne returned his gaze candidly, her eyes never wavering from their brown target. One advantage to dark glasses, she thought. I can read his expression, but he can't read mine.

Then she let her eyes flit over the thick hair that lay in soft curls around his face, black and shining, gleaming like burnished metal in the sunlight. His shoulders were broad and straight, filling out the material of the shirt, the muscles in his arms flexing as he lifted the glass to his lips.

She smiled when she recalled that she could see much more of him than he could of her, and he mistook

14

this for an admission that she was pleased by his greeting. But that's all right, she reflected when his smile widened. She did approve of him. Outdoorsy. Tough. Physical.

Yet she could see the subtle signs of sophistication. Though dressed casually, she could tell that his clothes were costly. Practically no jewelry, but what there was, was unquestionably expensive—a wristwatch, and that small gold chain around his neck, half-hidden in a mat of springy black curls.

Now she did smile at him. It was that smile that tantalized everyone who saw it; it was that smile that made them her willing slaves. It began as a tiny twitch of the lips, burgeoning into happiness on her face, ending up with those luminous eyes, now safely hidden from view.

He tensed, still waiting. She was in no hurry, he thought. Taking her time! If only he could see her eyes, he silently muttered in exasperation, he'd know what she was thinking. He'd know how to react. The smile, though, was encouraging. Would she do more? Did she want more?

She saw the consternation furrowed on his face, and she almost chuckled. She lifted the glass. . . . He caught his breath. . . . He thought it was a signal, but she touched her lips instead to the straw and sipped her drink. She enjoyed creating this suspense. No need to let him know too soon that she liked him. Keep him in the dark a little longer!

The tactic wasn't new. Women all over the world had used it, he seethed. But he didn't like one using it on him. Suddenly he went through an elaborate pantomine of being uninterested, flicking his wrist, casually looking down at his watch, signaling to the waiter. Out of the corner of his eyes he spared her a furtive glance.

He smiled to himself. She looked surprised. Good! He kept his exultation to himself; he didn't dare let it reach his lips. Now it was his turn to watch concern leave its imprint on her face.

Had she dallied too long, she wondered, jabbing her straw into her drink, smashing the ice. She couldn't afford to act too quickly, she admonished herself, lowering her head, pursing her lips, sucking on the straw, and peering at him over the rims of her glasses. But again, she reasoned, she was gambling and could very well lose him.

If he looks up one more time . . .

The brown eyes again looked directly at her. He would give her one more chance, and his eyes told her this. But, even then, she didn't move too hastily. Not good to let him know just how much he was affecting her. She pulled the straw out of her mouth, lifted the glass in his direction, and nodded.

"Hello," she said softly, the sound barely carrying over to his table.

He continued to stare, not rising to his feet instantly. Was she used to having men make passes at her like this? Was this an everyday occurrence? As many times as he'd been through this maneuver, he didn't like the idea of her going through it with another man. He found the thought wholly unsavory. He pushed the chair back with the full weight of his body and slowly stood up, each movement thoroughly planned and executed.

He was coming! Her heart beat faster, the pulse pounding erratically at her neck, her wrists, throughout her body, her blood rushing wildly through her veins. She began to breathe faster, a little more labored than usual, and she felt that film of nervous moisture that beaded in the palms of her hands, on her upper lip, and on her forehead.

Behave, Francyne, she rebuked herself sharply, her fingers running across her upper lip and her brow. After all, you're not some starry-eyed teenager. You're a grown woman. Almost twenty-eight. Behave like a woman, not a child! An enigmatic smile began to tug at her full lips. Some other time, her romantic self responded, pushing reason aside with no second thought. Right now I'm going to enjoy being with this male.

She watched as he took the few steps that brought him to her table. She liked the brown-toned shirt, cottony soft, veed lower at the neck because he hadn't buttoned it all the way up, sleeves rolled up so that his forearms were exposed. Sinewy, she thought appreciatively. Strong fingers curled around the glass of scotch. Expensive jeans. His thick, muscular thighs stretched the material taut as he moved his legs. She liked what she saw, all the way down to the toes of his boots, which gleamed a rich, rusty brown.

Then he was at the table, her eyes were on the same level as his arms, and she saw the dark hair that curled on his forearms, wrists, the upper joint of each finger. She was especially impressed with his fingers, strong, with carefully clipped nails. As if mesmerized, she could lift her eyes no higher. She watched the other hand, those same strong fingers closing over the back of the chair. She heard the coarse grating of the legs on the saltillo tile floor.

The voice was huskily resonant, altogether a pleasant sound. "Hello, I'm Brendan O'Shea."

Her eyes were riveted on his face, on those brown eyes, dark and fathomless, eyes that seemed to be laughing at her. But they gleamed with pleasure; he was glad that she had invited him to join her. She could read no more than this. It was as if he had lowered invisible shutters over his eyes that protected his thoughts and emotions from her scrutiny.

My cue, she decided, disappointed by his retreat. As a result she didn't remove her sunglasses, not wanting to let him see into her thoughts either. She opened her mouth to speak, but the sound didn't come. She swallowed and tried again.

"Francyne LaRue." She was surprised. It sounded like her voice. If she hadn't known better, she would have thought she was cool, calm, and collected.

"Tourist?"

She shook her head. "Not exactly." She paused. "Although some would say so." Thinking of Norma, she dimpled. "Actually I'm a lifetime resident of the Alamo City, even though I continue to act like a tourist." She shrugged her shoulders; her smile widened. "Guess that's why I work for a tourist agency."

"Tour guide?" he asked, his brows lifted inquiringly.

She shook her head. "No, travel advisor." Succinctly she described her duties as manager of the agency and answered the questions that he inserted at appropriate intervals. "How about you?"

He didn't answer immediately; instead he motioned the waiter and ordered another scotch and water, asking that his lunch be served at her table.

"I work for a national hardware and lumber company," he said, mentioning the name of the firm. But he volunteered no more.

"What are you doing on the river?" she asked, feeling uninhibited and not embarrassed to pry. "Is your office near here?"

He shook his head, smiling, his fingers busily engaged in wiping the condensation from his glass. "No, my office isn't around here. I was just transferred, and I'm living in the Palacio del Rio until I get into an apartment."

"You haven't found one yet?" Francyne asked with mild interest.

He nodded. "Found one. I'm going to move in next week. Care to help me?"

Francyne casually shrugged her shoulders, thinking the question was a trifle premature. She lowered her head and sipped at her drink.

"Well?" he prodded. He wanted to hear her answer, if only out of curiosity.

Francyne lifted her head and looked at him, no trace of amusement on her face. Finally, however, the corners of her lips twitched, and she asked softly, "I suppose you have some etchings you want me to see also?"

He grinned. "No, I'm not an etcher." He placed both arms on the table, cupping his glass in his hands. "I do like to decorate my own apartment though." He laughed. "I went through the interior-decorator bit once, and I've never forgotten it." Without explaining further, he added, "Since I'm the one who's going to live there, I want to choose each item that goes into it."

Francyne laughed, remembering when she'd gone shopping to fit out her first apartment. "I know what you mean. When I moved out on my own, my mother and my sister decided to help me decorate. Of course, they both wanted me to end up with the type of apartment that each of them wanted." She chuckled. "We almost got into a knock-down-drag-out, but I finally convinced them that the apartment was mine and that I should have the privilege of filling it with whatever I pleased."

He watched her face when she talked. He liked the excitement that filtered through; he liked the way her mouth curved when she smiled. He wondered about her eyes, though. What were they like? Did they sparkle and dance when she talked? What color were they?

"What kind of apartment do you have?"

Francyne mulled over the question, then said, "I live in a small complex off Broadway. Two bedrooms, large living-dining area, and a kitchen with a breakfast nook."

"Live by yourself?"

Francyne nodded. "Didn't at first! But I soon found out that I could depend on myself to pay the bills better than I could worry about someone else forgetting to pay her bills."

"How's it decorated?" He would get a description of her, he thought.

"Bright splashy colors in the kitchen," she replied. "Soothing colors in the living room and bedroom." She smiled as she admitted, "I'm rather homey. I like to be comfortable. I've got some old pieces from the house mixed in with my new furniture." She laughed, pulling a face. "I guess you can call it Early Francyne."

He smiled, his eyes lingering on her lips, which so easily moved with her smile. "That's what it ought to be, a portrait of its owner. I'd like to see it."

Abruptly she changed the subject. "What kind of work do you do?"

He lifted the glass to his lips, hiding the smile that still lurked there. How's that for a quick manuever? he thought. He sipped the scotch.

"Administrative," he returned evasively. "I'm one of the guys the big shots send to places that no one else wants to go to." He laughed. "They even put a vice-whatever in front of my name, so I can't refuse to go."

"And what's so unsavory about coming to San Antonio?" Francyne asked defensively.

Again he laughed. "Nothing really. I just had roots in Baton Rouge, and it was tough pulling up stakes and moving."

She nodded. "Here for long?"

"Probably so," he answered ruefully. "I'll probably be here until we have this divisional office all set up." Tired of discussing his job, he changed the subject. "No more about business," he announced flatly, leaning forward, propping his elbows on the table, resting his chin in the palms of his hands. "I want to enjoy this time that I'm spending with you, and I don't want to discuss work anymore—yours or mine. Okay?"

"Okay," she agreed, a little breathlessly. "What do you want to talk about?" She hoped the heavy thudding of her heart wasn't apparent to him.

"For starters," he said, that special warmth of his eyes spilling onto her, burning her like molten gold. "I'd like to know more about you."

Francyne picked up her glass; she needed to have something to do with her hands so he wouldn't notice her nervousness. But she didn't lift it to her lips. Instead she ran her fingers up and down the stem.

"Francyne LaRue. Twenty-seven, soon to be twenty-eight. One of two children. The younger of two daughters. Sister to Sophia Major, whom we call Sophie. Aunt to Keeley Francyne Major, an eleven-year-old urchin whom I adore. Daughter of John and Sylvia LaRue. Born and raised in San Antonio. Ten years with Travel Texas-Style." She paused thoughtfully. "That's about it."

"You've left out the most important fact," he said dryly, picking up her left hand, gazing at the fourth finger. "Not married?" He raised his eyes, staring into her face, looking for her answer.

21

"No," she whispered softly, loving the feel of those strong fingers on her soft ones.

"Ever been married?"

She shook her head.

"Boyfriend?"

"Yes," she nodded. "A boyfriend."

The answer didn't please him. "Serious?"

Suddenly he dropped his guard, and the shutter raised. She could read his thoughts. He was interested, and he wanted to know. It was more than idle curiosity.

"A good friend," she answered truthfully, wondering why she would confess this to a total stranger—wondering why she wanted to tell him that Sterling Blair was the friend she used when she wanted to drive off unwanted males, a friend who actually was a friend, a boyfriend where other men were concerned.

He smiled. "Good! I'd hate to break his heart."

She smiled, her eyes never leaving his face. "What makes you think you'd break his heart?" Again she felt that dizzy sensation; she felt as if her body and her soul were separated, and a part of her was floating somewhere above herself, in herself, out of herself, around herself.

"When I take you away from him."

"Sure of yourself," she parried, enjoying their game.

Now he laughed, not deigning to answer too quickly, his eyes taking on an enigmatic shine that was sensual, caressing. "I'm sure" came the quiet reply.

She laughed, the sound soft and husky. "Surely I have something to say about this?"

"Since you're nothing but good friends," he countered suavely, his fingers gently massaging hers all the while, "the question remains hypothetical."

"Right," she conceded, liking his audacity but still pulling her hand free from his evocative grasp. "Now tell me something about yourself," she commanded gently, but firmly. "I've given you my vital statistics. It's your turn now."

He nodded his head. "Brendan O'Shea. Thirty-five. Not married. Never been married. No steady girl. One sister, Joan. Two ex-brothers-in-law. One prospective brother-in-law. One father, Brian O'Shea. One step-mother. One mother, Leslie I'm-not-so-sure-what-her-last-name-is-now. Three ex-stepfathers. Forgot their names. Born and raised in Baton Rouge. Transferred to San Antonio." His lips quirked, and he smiled intimately at her, the warmth of his eyes melting some far, secret corner inside her. "Since I don't have a girl-friend, I wonder if you'd have any suggestions."

"None," Francyne replied, tongue-in-cheek. "I'll give it some thought though."

"How about you?"

She chuckled. "Got any personal references?" She lifted her eyebrows above the rim of her glasses.

"None." His eyes snapped with pleasure. "That's why I need your help. I need to build up my romantic credit line."

Francyne slowly shook her head, her expression half-mocking, half-serious. "Not my cup of tea."

"If you don't grab me," he warned, "it may be too late."

Now she smiled. Persistent devil! "I'll just have to take that chance!"

Below the bantering remarks, he sensed her caution, and he understood. Perhaps he even admired her. Right now, however, he wasn't too sure. He hated being thwarted, even though the reason might be justifiable. But he knew when to change the subject.

"You work nearby here?"

Francyne suppressed a smile of triumph. She pointed. "Over there. On street level." She turned and gazed at the river. "From my office I can see the river." She propped an elbow on the table and cupped her chin in the palm of her hand, curling her fingers over her mouth. In a muffled voice she said, "I love this old river and its city."

With indolent grace Brendan turned from the waist and looked uninterestedly at the river. "What's so special about it?"

Francyne could hear the dry sarcasm in his question. She smiled. How many times had she heard this same question. How many times had she heard the same skepticism.

Succinctly she began to tell him the story of the city by the winding river. Her voice carried him beyond the splash of the water to the history that flowed with it. She told him about the richness of its heritage; she talked of the city that arose on the far frontier of two great colonial empires—Great Britain's and Spain's; she described the uniquely American culture that emerged from these two.

Caught up in her story, believing her story, Francyne made the bare historical facts come alive, and he listened with rapt attention, loving the sound of her voice, liking the animation on her face, the dancing cadence of her Texas drawl, her excitement and exuberance. He did wish she'd take those blasted glasses off. Not seeing her eyes took away from the completeness of his pleasure and enjoyment.

"There's no place on earth as beautiful as San Antonio," she concluded, taking a deep breath, leaning back in her chair.

"Ever been anywhere else?" he asked with feigned detachment, enthralled with this creature sitting across from him.

24

She laughed, not the least bit put out by his cynicism. "Not really," she replied. "I've been through most of the southern states, the Southwest, and California, but," she added emphatically, fully catching his insinuation and not easily conceding that he could be right in his criticism, "I still think San Antonio was special."

"Would I meet your standard of approval if I say at this point that there are some very wonderful and special things in San Antonio?" His eyes caressed her.

"Perhaps," she replied, smiling almost shyly, retreating from the suggestion of intimacy in those eyes. Every time he looked at her, she felt as if he'd touched her physically. She felt the velvety softness of his touch; she felt the sensual heat of the caress.

"Closer to the truth," he amended, knowing the effect he had on women and seeing the same response in Francyne that he'd seen in others, "there's someone very special in San Antonio."

Confident . . . *overly confident.* . . . He allowed his arrogance to gleam in the depth of his eyes, making no effort to conceal it. How many times had he charmed a woman with this line? Innumerable!

Francyne saw the flinty arrogance in his eyes, and she resented it. Think it, she silently screamed, but don't throw it in my face. Give me some credit for having intelligence! The dreamy, faraway look quickly disappeared.

"I'm sure you find someone special, no matter where you may be." She smiled demurely, letting him know she had read as well as heard the message. Both meanings!

Still preoccupied with her glasses, which she had still not taken off, and slightly annoyed by her cool, effective riposte, he suddenly asked, "Nearsighted?"

This was too much. She was seething. "Yes! Why?" The words came out cold and terse. Not too much could put a dent in her good humor, but this coming from an arrogant stranger really irritated her. She'd been wearing glasses long enough that she wasn't self-conscious about them, but his question did rankle. Why? She couldn't put her finger on it. But for the first time in her life she wished that she didn't have to wear them.

He shrugged and moved uncomfortably in his chair, instantly aware of her withdrawal and irritation. He tried to correct his error without calling too much attention to his callousness.

"Since you've kept them on all the time we've been talking, I figured you must be. Nearsighted people are affected more by glare and sunlight than others."

Francyne didn't reply. At that moment the waiter brought their meal, and she applied all her attention to the sandwich and chips. If she had tried to speak, her voice would have probably been shaky. Again she asked herself why. And again she couldn't give herself a plausible answer. You'd think, Francyne LaRue, she admonished, trying to swallow a bite that grew larger and larger, that a woman your age would know better.

She wasn't ordinarily this sensitive. She took another bite of her sandwich, her eyes hardly straying past the perimeter of her plate. Why should this man—Brendan O'Shea—this stranger, affect her so deeply, so quickly? Did she already like him too much? Maybe! Maybe, my foot! she rebuked herself. Why else do you care what he thinks about your wearing glasses!

She kept chewing, and the lump of tunafish grew and grew. She could hardly swallow it. Got to eat, she thought, trying to hold on to her outward appearance. Can't let him see how he's affecting me. She finally

26

managed to swallow the lump, washing it down with a large swallow of water.

She managed to eat a few bites from the other half of the sandwich. Good, she thought. At least it looks like I might be finished. Got to get away from here before I make a fool of myself. She twisted her wrist, glancing at her watch. He would think it was time for her to return to the office.

Brendan noticed it all: her cool withdrawal, her rigid motions and tense silence, her preoccupation with her food, the hand that flitted up to her sunglasses every now and then. He breathed deeply, still annoyed with himself for having made her self-conscious. Suddenly he wasn't hungry either; he threw down his fork, wiped his mouth with his napkin, and crumpled it up. He took a large gulp of cold water and leaned back in the chair, studying Francyne, trying to figure her out.

His eyes narrowed, and he stared pensively at her. Why was he finding it so difficult to reach her? Why did he have to be so clumsy? He'd never had trouble in the past. He'd never retaliated with such a trite remark. In fact, he thought, women generally flung themselves at him. And now this Miss Tourist Guide outrageously ignored him. She had completely tuned him out of existence.

"I'm sorry," he said softly. "I didn't mean to offend you. I just wanted to see the color of your eyes." He tried to find that humorous streak that he felt must be lurking behind that cool aloofness. "I wanted to see if they matched the rest of you."

Silently she looked up to peruse his face, and when she reached the conclusion that he was telling the truth, she put her half-eaten sandwich on the plate, wiped her hands on the napkin, and carefully tucked it under the side of her dish.

27

With deliberately slow motions she raised her right hand, enclosed the round plastic frames with her thumb and first two fingers, and slipped off her glasses, setting them down on top of the napkin.

"Hazel," she said flatly. "Kind of tempermental. They change colors depending on what I'm wearing. And my mood, some say."

She was right, he thought, looking at her eyes for the first time, taking pleasure in their beauty. They were an unusual color. Now they looked blue, and hidden deeply in their recesses were golden flecks that from time to time danced ephemerally in the sunshine. Yet, at the same time, they weren't blue. They just appeared to be. Elusive, he decided with lingering delight. Chimerical, like the woman!

"Do they?" she asked quietly, waiting for his reply. Her lips, wide and sensuous, were innocently parted in a provocative smile, the small teeth gleaming brilliantly.

Her words broke the spell that bound him. "Do they?" he repeated inanely, blinking his eyes, glancing into her face questioningly.

"Do they match the rest of me?" she asked softly.

"They do," he returned just as softly, his words almost a whisper, his eyes missing the amusement that flickered on Francyne's face. He was too absorbed in the total effect that she was creating at the moment. He didn't want to break the spell. His eyes raked over the white silk blouse, the blue and white scarf, the red straw bag that lay on the table. He more than liked what met his eyes. He wanted to see—to learn, to explore, to discover—what didn't meet the eye. "Would you like to have dinner with me tonight?"

The amusement slowly crept into her eyes. "Can't, she replied.

"Can't or won't?" The words lashed across the table with the cracking precision of a whip.

Francyne smiled. "You choose."

It was time someone whittled this man down to size, she decided, not bothering to disguise her thoughts. Evidently he was accustomed to getting his way *whenever* he wanted his way. On the other hand, she was independent enough that she wasn't accustomed to answering to someone else.

She saw the disappointment in his eyes. She began to toy with the stem of her glass. "I have other plans for tonight."

This time the words were as soft as an endearment, calculated to compel obedience. "Cancel them."

With no hesitation she shook her head. "I wouldn't do that."

His eyes narrowed, and he unknowingly dropped that invisible shutter that closed his mind from hers. Was she lying to him? Was this a grand put-off? God, he seethed, if it was, he didn't like the feeling at all!

"Your friend?" he asked, hoping it wasn't, watching her closely. Suddenly he felt the horrible constriction as jealously wrapped its tenacles around his brain, squeezing out all rational thought.

"No." It wasn't a sound at all, just a small sigh that drifted across the table.

Why didn't she let him believe that she had a date? she wondered hazily. Why did she feel compelled to tell him the truth? Just because she had seen the disappointment on his face?

Again the soft, seductive cajoling: "And you can't cancel your plans?"

"No," she replied, not retfeating from her denial. "I can't."

He nodded, recognizing the ring of truth in her answer, knowing that further argument was futile. "I understand." But he didn't, not in this case. Why couldn't she want to be with him as much as he wanted to be with her? "Will I see you again?" The question was distasteful to him. Generally he was the one being asked, not the one doing the asking.

"Do you want to?" she parried, her eyes seeking out the truth in his.

"Yes." When he saw her eyes light up, when he saw that smile travel rapidly from her eyes to her lips, he added, "Introduce me to your city." She nodded, laughter and joy leaping in her eyes. "But not tonight?"

"Not tonight," she repeated. The answer was soft, but he heard the ring of decision in it. Then she lowered her face, picked up her purse, and dug for her wallet.

When she began to count her money and put it down on the ticket, his big hand settled over her smaller one. "Let me get this for you?"

"No, thanks" came the gentle answer. "I pay my way unless I'm asked out."

"I'd like to," he insisted.

"Another time."

"What about your address and phone number?" he asked, knowing she had deliberately avoided giving them to him.

"Not right now," she replied easily, standing up. She tucked her purse under her arm and slipped her dark glasses over her eyes once again. "I want to know you better first."

Her refusal went against the grain. He wasn't accustomed to being turned down. "When will I see you again?"

She heard the sardonic mockery in his voice, and she knew he was trying to belittle her. It won't work, she thought, hiding her smile. I've played this river pick-up game too many times.

"I'll meet you for lunch Monday." Take it or leave it, she silently enjoined. I've been through too many of these casual encounters, and I don't intend to be victimized again.

Taking out his wallet, he counted out the bills and laid them on his check; then he followed her through the maze of tables until they reached the cobblestone walkway. He didn't speak again until they had moved away from the crowd and were walking down the river.

"I believe in women's lib, Francyne—" he began, a hint of disdain in his voice. But even with that it was the first time that she'd heard him use her name, and she liked it. She loved those husky, vibrant tones that felt like velvet to her senses, rubbing them, caressing them, polishing them.

"—but I like being the one to ask for dates. I like being the one to initiate things."

Again Francyne suppressed a smile. She would have to be content to let her happiness leap in her eyes, safely protected by the smoky-gray lenses. She was amused at his displeasure, his discomfort at finding she'd taken control. But she was elated that he wanted to see her again. The thought thoroughly warmed her.

"You can understand that?" he demanded, the brown eyes hard and firm in their appeal.

Honesty was her only choice, she decided, licking her lips nervously. "Since I live by myself, I don't give my number out . . . indiscriminately."

"A very wise practice." The words were without sarcasm or criticism, yet they were cool.

"I . . . I . . ." Her voice had dropped to an embarassed murmur, and Brendan could hardly hear the low, husky tones. "I'm not a pick-up."

He stopped walking, grabbed her hand, and pulled her off the walkway onto the grass. He stared into her face with stupefaction. How little she trusted men! A variety of emotions rushed through him, first anger, then perplexity, then amusement. Last, a surging desire to sweep her into his arms and kiss her until her glasses fell off, until she melted into him.

Not too fast, he admonished himself in that split second. Tread softly or you'll lose her. Try for lightness. He smiled, the corners of his mouth twitching, red-hot embers smoldering in his dark eyes. He caught both her hands in his.

"I know you're not a pick-up." He laughed softly. "If I don't know the difference between a truck and a woman by now, I'm certainly in a mess."

She didn't laugh. Not even a smile! So much for that! Try again.

Softer came the words: "I know the difference between women and *women.*"

Still no response from Francyne. He gave up! He acquiesced. Might as well if he wanted to see her again. Right now it was like talking to a statue, a cold, lifeless, uncaring statue.

"All right, Francyne—"

She couldn't help but hear the steely promise as he slowly and emphatically enunciated each word. She knew that this was no idle threat. He meant what he said!

"—I'll meet you here for lunch Monday, but then I want your address and phone number. I want to call you, talk to you, visit with you. Okay?"

She nodded, looking bemusedly at her hands, which he still held captive in his. Without his being aware of it, his fingertips were gently fondling her wrist, the sensitive area just above the palm of her hand. She shivered with the delightful sensations that ran unchecked through her body. She didn't want this feeling to stop; she didn't want him to stop. But, then again, she didn't want him to know how much he was affecting her.

She inhaled sharply, looking into his face and nodding assent, never thinking of pulling her hands away. Satisfied with her answer, he tugged at her wrists, and they resumed their walk. Even then, however, he only let go of one hand. Too soon, she thought, they reached that flight of stairs that would take her to street level.

"This is where I get off," she told him, wishing her lunch hour weren't over, wishing she didn't have to leave him. She pointed to the building that housed her office. "That's where I work." She smiled. "I'll see you Monday. Same time, same place!"

He nodded, reluctant to let her go. His hand still gently clasped hers in its warmth, and she felt the latent strength in his fingers. He refused to turn her loose. He refused to part with her one second sooner than he had to.

"Francyne—"

She heard the pleading in his voice.

"—if you should change your mind about tonight—"

She shook her head, but he ignored this, hoping it was only a motion of her head and not her heart.

"If you should decide to cancel your plans—"

Her heart did say yes, but she still shook her head.

"I'll be waiting. I'll be on the terrace of the hotel."

She was standing on the lower step; he stood below her on the walkway. Dropping her hand, he backed away, his feet making a muffled sound on the cobblestones. His dark gaze, intimate and caressing, washed over her once again as he drank in every aspect of her loveliness. He willed her to cancel her plans, to come with him instead.

She opened her mouth to speak, but no words would come. She stood perfectly still, hesitating to leave him, dreading to return to the office. *What if he didn't meet her on Monday? Sophie would understand! I could call; she could work something out.*

"I . . . I . . . " She stammered, wanting to meet him, but also struggling with her conscience. *Sophie was depending on her. It was too late for Sophie to arrange something else now.*

He heard the hesitation in her voice, he felt her indecision, and he pressed the advantage.

"Remember," he said softly. "I'll be waiting on the terrace." He glanced at his watch. "Say about seven."

"I don't know," she said wretchedly, her mind racing ahead, trying to find a way to keep her promise to Sophie and still meet him there. *Not possible,* she concluded. *Mom won't be home until Sunday. What would you do with Keeley while you're here with him?* Again she shook her head, this time more firmly. "I can't."

He nodded, hearing the words and the dull thud of finality that accompanied them. Yet all the while he hoped she would change her mind.

"I'll be waiting."

CHAPTER TWO

Since they were going to be eating on the river, Francyne dressed casually in a green-and-white striped blouse and white denim knickers. She was having a problem, however, deciding how to wear her hair. First she clipped it back with barrettes, but she didn't like that. Next she pinned it in a loose knot at the nape of her neck. She stepped back to survey the effect. Nope, that wouldn't do either!

"What's he like, Franny?"

Francyne dropped the pins on the dresser and looked at the eleven-year-old girl who was sprawled in the middle of the bed, kicking her legs up and down in the air, noisily munching on an apple.

What am I going to do? she wondered, answering Keeley's question absently. "Tall . . . black hair . . . brown eyes." She fiddled with the combs, the barrettes again, a ribbon.

"What else?" Keeley snorted disgustedly. The little girl jabbed her index finger between her freckled

35

cheeks, accurately hitting the nosepiece of her glasses, giving them a shove up her pixie nose.

Francyne brushed her hair, pulled it back, braided it, unbraided it, twisted it into a knot, untwisted it, and finally stood looking at herself in the mirror, sighing. Why not be drastically different? she quipped to herself, sweeping one side back over her ear, holding it in place with a comb.

"Is he good-looking?" Keeley demanded, not easily sidetracked or ignored, her blue eyes riveted on her aunt's image in the mirror.

"Sort of," Francyne murmured, not hearing the question, preoccupied with her hair at the moment.

"You're not even listening to me," Keeley complained softly. "Seems to me like you're really trying to impress this guy who's sorta good-looking." She giggled when Francyne cast her a reproving glare. Keeley's voice then became mushy with romantic sentiment. "Is he a hunk, Francyne?"

Her attention on her hair once again, Francyne didn't immediately respond. She opened one of the dresser drawers and pulled out a green scarf. Would it match? Yes, she thought, holding it up to the blouse. This is it! She looped it around her head. I'll tie my hair back from my face with this. Cool and casual, bringing the green around my forehead. She adjusted the collar of her blouse. Very good! Pleased with the effect, she twirled in front of the mirror.

Patiently Keeley repeated her question, dry sarcasm coating the words. "I said, Francyne, is he a hunk?"

Francyne slid her long slender foot into a pair of green-canvas wedge-heeled shoes and transferred her things from the red straw bag to a canvas tote bag.

"Well," Keeley demanded, not so patiently this time, still determined to receive an answer, "is he?"

"Yes," Francyne muttered, again not really hearing the question, but answering out of habit and endeavoring to keep Keeley happy, or at least pacified. She slung the tote bag over her shoulder, surveying the total image. "How do I look, Keeley?" She pirouetted in front of the full-length mirror on the closet door.

Keeley sat up, folding her legs in front of her, carefully studying her aunt. "Okay, I guess," she finally replied. "What are ya'll gonna do tonight?"

Francyne moved back to the dresser and selected a pair of glasses that suited her outfit. Setting them on her nose, she said, "We're going to eat on the river, and maybe later we'll go to Sunken Gardens."

"Ugh," Keeley grunted, "that sounds boring. When I grow up and start dating, I'm gonna do more exciting things than go to a park." Thoroughly disenchanted with the subject and disappointed with her aunt, Keeley scooted to the edge of the bed and dropped her apple core into the wastepaper basket. About that time the doorbell chimed. "Bet that's Lisa," she called over her shoulder, scampering into the living room. A little later she shouted, "Franny, it's Lisa."

Francyne, satisfied with her appearance, walked into the living room, dropping her bag into the nearest chair. She cast an amused glance at the slender blonde wearing faded cutoffs and an oversized T-shirt who was standing in the doorway with two large grocery bags tucked in the crook of her arms.

"Moving in?" she asked with an impish grin.

"Not quite," Lisa retorted in the same spirit, strolling toward the kitchen. "I just wanted to be prepared. This is my first time baby-sitting with Keeley, and I didn't want to come up short. Keeley and I have an evening of televiewing ahead of us, and I didn't want to run out of goodies."

"We won't run out," Keeley promised her. "Franny's got all kinds of food in the refrigerator, Cokes, pies, cookies, sandwiches." She grabbed one of the bags. "Let me help you."

Francyne shook her head and smiled as the girls carried the bags into the kitchen. "No studies?" she called, noticing that Lisa hadn't brought any books.

"Yeah," Lisa replied unenthusiastically, opening the refrigerator door. "I need to study for final exams. No big deal! I'm on top of everything."

"I'll bet," Francyne commented dryly.

Lisa returned to the living room, slapping her hands against her jeans. She grinned. "You sound just like Joyce, and she sounds just like Mom."

"I think your sister and I understand you quite well," Francyne replied matter-of-factly, glancing at her watch.

Keeley, who had been occupied with unloading the grocery bags, now raced into the living room, her face shining with anticipation and excitement. She danced around the room.

"Oh, Franny," she giggled, "I'm gonna have so much fun tonight. Baby-sit me again so I can have a baby-sitter like Lisa. Momma gets baby-sitters who aren't any fun like this. All they want to do is talk to their boyfriends on the telephone."

"Keeley, there's not another one like you in the world." Francyne chuckled, grabbing her niece in a tight bear hug. "Come to think of it, I couldn't stand another one." She grinned into the impish face that was turned up to her. "I love you to death, brat." Then she asked, "What makes you think Lisa won't be talking on the telephone tonight?"

Keeley danced out of Francyne's arms. "Because I asked her if she had a boyfriend, and she said yes, but he went home this weekend. So . . ." She droned to a halt, smiling triumphantly.

Lisa chuckled. "I see that I've got my hands full tonight."

" 'Fraid so," Francyne agreed, walking to the chair, slinging her purse over her shoulder. "Guess I'll be running along now. See you later." She turned to Lisa. "Do you have everything that you'll need?"

Lisa nodded. "If not, Joyce will be next door to help me." Francyne nodded. "Did you leave me any phone numbers in case I need to reach you?"

"On the pad by the phone in the bedroom," Francyne replied.

"That's it then," Lisa said, pursing her lips pensively, running her fingers through the short mass of thick curls that bobbed around her face. "Guess that covers it."

But Francyne didn't think so. She stood in the door and regaled them with a long list of do's and don'ts. She began with "Be sure to lock the door, and . . ." The list seemed unending. Finally Lisa interrupted her, gently shoving her out the door.

"Okay, Mother Hen, I read you. You can go now. Keeley and I can take care of ourselves. If not, Joyce is close enough." She pointed to the adjacent apartment.

Francyne laughed with them and walked out of the building toward her car. Excitement welled up in waves until her stomach felt as if it were turning over. She had to admit, though, it had been a long, long time since she had looked forward to a date so much. A long time indeed!

In the car she turned on the radio, letting the soft music soothe her before she saw Brendan again. Because she had driven the route so many times, she could let her mind run wild with delicious thoughts of him and the evening ahead, taking no thought of her driving. Finally she drove in front of the hotel, slid out, let the valet park her car, and walked to the river.

Gracefully she walked down the stone steps to the river, scanning the crowd with each step she took, looking for that familiar face. When she didn't immediately see him in the group of people who were seated in front of the hotel, her heart slowed down until she thought it would stop beating altogether, and she felt an undefinable hurt in her chest. Surely he wouldn't stand her up! Out of sight, out of mind!

Then she saw him, leaning indolently on the stone bridge that spanned the river close to the hotel. At the distance she couldn't see his eyes, but she could feel his gaze fixed upon her as she walked closer. She could feel the warmth that licked across her body like a brushfire. How little it would take to be enveloped in those flames.

Her lips lifted in a smile at the same time that his hand came up in a wave. He returned the smile, slowly straightened, and started moving in her direction. He was glad to see her, and he was pleasantly surprised by the casual elegance of her attire. He was beside her, his hand cupped her elbow, and he guided her to one of the patio tables.

"Hello," he said softly, sliding a chair out for her. "I was wondering if you'd stand me up or not." He sat down, gazing across the table, glad that she wasn't wearing her shades, wanting to look at her eyes. What color were they now?

Francyne smiled. "No, that's not my style. I'm a woman of my word."

The waiter stood by the table, ready to take their order for cocktails.

"What are you in the mood for tonight, Francyne?"

40

Brendan's words, seductive in their implications, made Francyne's imagination run wild. She could have sworn there was a double meaning to the question. Goes to prove that you're nervous and sensitive, she pointed out to herself. Get yourself under control! The evening's just begun.

She smiled. "Lime daiquiri, please."

Brendan gave his order, and the waiter disappeared, leaving them to ponder the menu. "What would you like to eat?"

"Everything sounds good. I love food, period," she returned, her gaze lifting from the menu.

He grinned. "Are you always this easily pleased?"

She shrugged, feeling that shyness was getting the upper hand again. "Not always," she answered truthfully.

He couldn't tear his eyes from her face—from her eyes in particular. He searched their rich depths. "You were right," he eventually said.

Francyne quirked her brows inquiringly, but he didn't have time to answer. The waiter set their drinks in front of them, and took their order.

When they were alone again, Francyne asked, "Right about what?"

He lifted his glass and took a swallow of his scotch. "Your eyes." He lapsed into silence, leaning back in the chair, looking at them, still amazed at the startling change. Earlier today they had been a grayish blue, now they were green.

Again Francyne shrugged. "Hazel." She said the word as if it told the entire story. "They change color with whatever I wear." She pointed to the green in her blouse. "Green stripes, green eyes."

"They're beautiful."

"Thank you," she whispered, suddenly lowering her

head, afraid to allow herself to come any closer, afraid of the flames of passion that would leap up between them, afraid she'd be burned beyond recognition. She looked down at the mound of crushed ice in her glass.

Perhaps it would have been better if she hadn't come, she thought. She almost hadn't. She had almost passed this up to spend an evening in front of the TV with Keeley and a pizza. But Brendan had taken matters into his own hands and had expertly persuaded her to change her plans. She bit her lower lip, jabbing her straw into the ice, admitting to herself that it hadn't taken much persuasion. She had wanted to meet him all along.

When she had returned to the office, she attempted to slip into the normal routine of the working day, but she hadn't succeeded. Brendan O'Shea, who had pushed his way into her lunch, now pushed his way into her thoughts. He refused to be cast aside; he demanded attention.

She would find herself holding a file in her hands, leaning back in her chair, gazing out the window, daydreaming about him. She would remember those eyes, their warmth, their amorous promise. She would remember that crown of black curls, the elegant gold chain that circled his muscular neck, that nestled in that mat of springy black curls on his chest.

During one of these moments she had heard someone clear his throat and speak.

"May I come in? Your secretary said it would be all right."

Francyne spun around, dropping her file on the desk, the contents spilling out. She stared at the physical essence of her dreams, that face, those eyes, that infuriating grin, the smile which so easily and effortlessly lifted those sensuous lips.

He stepped into the room, moving steadily toward the chair in front of her desk. Again he drawled in that sonorous tone, "Am I interrupting something important?"

He had been standing in the door watching her long enough to know that she had been daydreaming, and his eyes, ribald with laughter, told her so. They defied her to lie. They laughed when she clumsily shuffled the loose papers into the file jacket.

Behind that mocking laughter, she saw the arrogant flames of triumph as they leaped in his eyes. He didn't even have the decency to hide his gloating, she thought, her ire rising by the second. How dare he come into her office and do this!

"Cat got your tongue?" he asked, ensconcing his large frame in the chair, casually crossing his legs, propping his elbows on the chair arms, bridging his fingers together.

"No," she blurted out without thinking, and she could have bitten her tongue off when she saw his lips curving upward in a broad grin.

She squirmed uncomfortably when she realized that he sensed her irritation. She clutched the desk with one hand, pulled her chair closer, and picked up the neglected file with the other hand, tossing it into the Out basket.

She forced herself to breath normally. Relax, she instructed herself. Smile! Don't let him get the best of you. Unconsciously she lifted her left hand to adjust her glasses, which framed two gray-blue eyes clouded with surprise and dismay. Collecting her thoughts, she left her hand poised there a moment, her index finger crooked over the top of her glasses, the ball of her thumb resting on the bottom of the frames.

"No," she finally answered again, this time more

calmly, "the cat doesn't have my tongue." Her voice sounded normal; her anger was under control. She wasn't sure about her other emotions though. "I'm just surprised to see you here."

"Shouldn't be," he returned easily, twisting his head around, looking around the room, taking it all in. "You knew that I'd be seeing you again, and you knew that I wasn't going to wait until Monday."

Francyne stared at him defiantly, arching her brows. "What do you propose to do about it?"

She had his attention now. He'd seen her office; it looked like her. Now he wanted to look at her again. He enjoyed the play of emotion on her face. She hadn't learned to hide it yet.

"This is a travel agency of sorts?"

"Of sorts?" Francyne echoed indignantly.

"I mean," he corrected with a maddening grin, "you furnish guides for tourists and the like?"

Francyne nodded; a glimmer of his intent was shining through. She asked, nonetheless, "What do you have in mind?" not giving him the satisfaction of trying to second-guess him.

"Well," he said, uncrossing his legs, "it's like this. I'm not exactly a tourist, but I'm certainly unfamiliar with your fair city. I need to know it better. You know—"

She hardly heard the words. She was dazzled by his smile. It intrigued her. She liked those beautifully white teeth. They gleamed each time that his lips curved upward. The mellowness of his voice did something to her nerves. It was deeply masculine yet at the same time it was tender and gentle. She tuned in again, listening to the words, making herself hear more than the sounds.

44

"—we country people don't know how to act when we hit the city."

Francyne managed a shaky chuckle. "Country people, my foot!" she scoffed. "You're from Baton Rouge, and that's a far cry from the country."

He shrugged, enjoying her bantering tone. "Same difference. Well, what do you say?"

She widened her eyes innocently and stared at him with a blank expression. She presented an altogether alluring picture to the man across from her. She knew what he wanted, but she would make him spell it out.

"Say to what?"

He grinned, admiring her ability to score. "May I secure your services for this afternoon, tonight, and the weekend?"

Her eyes glowed with excitement. "I'm not a tourist guide," she gently pointed out, picking up her pencil and doodling idly on the pad in front of her. "Furthermore," she continued, not looking at him, "I'm off on the weekend. Even if I were to agree to be your guide" —she looked up at him, dropping her pencil on the desk—"I couldn't this weekend." She smiled. "I'm baby-sitting."

"All weekend?"

She nodded.

"With whom?" he asked, not caring that he was prying.

"Keeley," she repeated, also not caring. "My sister Sophie and her husband are going to Houston for a convention this weekend, and I'm keeping the urchin." The tenderness in her voice conveyed the depth of her love for the child. "It's too late for Sophie to get another baby-sitter, and Mom and Dad are out of town." She shrugged. "So I'm the logical choice."

Brendan knew that under the circumstances and at

the last minute Francyne wouldn't change her mind. She wouldn't budge from her decision to look after her niece. She would keep her word. This much he had figured out about her. It was up to him, then, to suggest a workable alternative.

"What are the two of you planning on doing?"

He wasn't interested in the answer; he was playing for time, time in which to plan and scheme, time in which to convince her to include him in her plans.

Francyne chuckled as she thought about her schedule for the next two days. "We're going to have one exciting weekend," she declared, her eyes dancing with devilish glints. "First thing tomorrow we're going to McDonald's for breakfast, then we're going to Aquarena Springs, and tomorrow night we're watching one of the late movies." She lifted her left hand, holding two fingers in the air. "We get to watch the reruns of two episodes of *Star Trek* at one time."

He grinned, thinking the weekend didn't sound that bad, realizing that he would be willing to do almost anything to spend more time with Francyne. Why? He didn't know, and he didn't take the time to analyze it now. He only knew that he was obsessed with the idea of knowing her better. She had insinuated herself into his being, and he wanted to know more about this woman who was too deeply imprinted on his thoughts and senses to be easily forgotten or pushed aside.

"What about including me in your day?" he asked, his brown eyes never leaving her face. "You could always use a man on the trip, couldn't you?"

She studied him, forcing herself to look relaxed. She reached for her pencil and clutched it nervously. "You don't think you'd find it boring?" she asked. Tensely she waited for the answer; she was tightly wound like a coil ready to spring loose at any moment.

"No, I don't think it would be boring."

She didn't think she could resist his argument much longer, and she knew that he wouldn't leave until he had won her over. She dropped her eyes, not allowing him to read her thoughts. She pushed her chair back. What would she do? What was she going to say? There was nothing . . . absolutely nothing . . . in the world that she would love any better than his going to San Marcos with them.

All the time he watched the expressions that flitted across her lowered face. He could guess at her thoughts.

"I like children," he added softly.

"I don't know," Francyne murmured. She stood up to walk over to the window and began to stare at the river as if the answer lay in its gentle ripples. After all, she told herself, she hadn't known him that long. He was virtually a stranger to her. She glanced over her shoulder, looking directly into those brown eyes, which were too familiar—too personal—for him to be a stranger.

He sensed her hesitancy, and he knew that she wanted to be with him. Taking advantage of her indecision, Brendan pressed her. "Are you by chance keeping Keeley this evening too?"

Nodding, Francyne turned to face him.

"Why not bring her with you and meet me for dinner?"

Why not? she thought. It would be ideal. Then, she remembered. She had promised Keeley that she could stay up for a late-night rerun of the movie *Dracula* on television.

Regretfully she said, "I don't think I can tonight. I promised Keeley that she could watch an old horror movie and—" She shrugged, almost apologetically, her voice lapsing into silence. After a while she said, "She's been looking forward to it all week and I promised her, and I hate to break my word to her."

Just as he figured! "Maybe you could get someone to sit with her tonight," he suggested, trying to keep a casual nonchalance in his voice.

Francyne shook her head. "I don't think so," she replied, then added, "If only Mom were home, but she's not. She and Dad are spending the week at Canyon Lake."

"No one else?"

Who could she get? she wondered. All of the baby-sitters that Sophie would recommend would be on her side of town and would do Francyne little good. And since she'd never had occasion to hire a baby-sitter, she didn't know where to begin at this late date.

"What about someone in your complex?"

She thought for a second, then her face brightened. Lisa Olson! Joyce's younger sister!

"Yes," she answered, "I know someone who might be willing to keep her this evening." She moved to the credenza behind her desk, tugging out the telephone book, and started thumbing through the pages. "She's attending UTSA and lives with her sister. I'm sure she would welcome the chance to earn some extra money." She began to dial. "That is if she doesn't have other plans." Impatiently she waited, listening to the intermittent ringing, wondering what she was letting herself in for. Finally she heard the click. "May I speak to Lisa?"

A brief conversation and the arrangements were set. Francyne chatted a little longer, unwilling to face Brendan again for some reason. Unwilling, she realized, to face the fact that she had been so easily, so artfully manipulated by him. Never before had a man had such an effect on her.

"That takes care of tonight," Brendan said when she finally hung up the phone. "What about the weekend?"

Francyne shrugged, appearing to be unconcerned. "Let's take it one day at a time, Brendan."

She saw the anger flare up in his eyes, but he didn't reply in kind. Instead he asked, "What time are you going to meet me?"

How he prided himself on having outmaneuvered her, she thought. But she didn't care. She'd let him know pretty soon just how much his machinations had accomplished.

"Seven."

"Seven," he repeated. "Sooner if possible."

Then he was gone, and Francyne finished her day in a daze.

"I'm glad you came," Brendan said, watching the bemused expression on her face, wondering what she had been thinking.

"I'm glad I came." Her eyes focused on the large hand that covered hers, looking at the small fine hair that shadowed the strong fingers.

They began to talk softly about themselves, sharing little secrets, learning about one another, laughing as they talked, lost in the small world they were creating. They ate, hardly noticing what they were eating, enjoying the spiritual essence of each other.

"I enjoy my work," Francyne explained in reply to one of his probing questions, "but I want more out of life than just a job."

His eyes narrowed, and he studied her. She could feel the cool disdain of his words. "You mean, you're one

49

of those women who won't be fulfilled until you're married and have babies."

Francyne thought for a minute, fully weighing this comment before she answered. His cynicism surprised as well as disappointed her. Slowly she shook her head.

"No, I'm not one of those women who feels compelled to get married and to have children. There are a lot of things I want to accomplish and experience first," she clarified, "but I do want to share my life with someone I love and raise our children together."

She smiled, thinking about her mom and dad, who had a wonderful marriage. In fact, thirty-five years worth, she remembered. And look at Sophie, she thought. She and Ron have been happily married for thirteen years.

"You're not single by choice?" Brendan asked.

She chuckled. "I'm single by choice today, but sometime in the future, when the right man comes along, I'll be a wife by choice."

He sipped his drink, listening to her, watching her hands move as she talked, watching her lips as they easily curved into a smile, watching the golden glints as they radiated from the center of her eyes outward through the colored irises.

"You sound as if you have something against marriage," she remarked, disliking that cynical gleam in his eyes and the derisive smirk on his face.

"I'm not an avid fan of the institution," he conceded. "To me it represents the end of a beautiful relationship in most cases."

"That's not true," Francyne argued, though her voice was soft. "My mom and dad have been married for thirty-five years, and they're happy. Sophie and Ron have been married for thirteen years, and both of them are happy." She smiled. "You can't condemn marriage just because of a few failures."

He laughed, the sound bitter and grating to Francyne's ears. "A few failures! In my family alone we have two professionals who've made careers of this blissful state of matrimony. My mother can proudly stand with the best, and Joan is quickly following in her footsteps."

"But all marriages aren't like that," Francyne protested.

"The ones I've seen haven't been too successful," Brendan countered coolly. "And if there are children, the children are caught in the middle. Generally the woman only keeps them because they're worth something in child support."

"Brendan!" Francyne cried in dismay, shocked at his angry skepticism. "How can you say that?"

He saw her eyes darken, and he felt her reproach. How many times had he encountered this reaction before. He'd stopped counting. Women who believed in marriage and wanted it tried to make him feel guilty about his attitude toward the whole subject. But he was indifferent to their reprimands, and he refused to feel guilty.

"I'm an authority on the subject of what happens to the children of divorced parents," he said acidly. "Believe me, I know. I was tossed back and forth between my mother and my father. Neither really wanted me when I was smaller. I was just the unplanned result of passion, and neither of them knew how to handle the remains of bygone love and romance." The last two words were harsh and bitter.

"I'm sorry," Francyne murmured, feeling his loneliness and despair, but not knowing how to empathize with him. Her childhood had been overflowing with love and unity. The family, their love, their support, had been a vital part of her developing years. She had never experienced rejection like his.

"Don't be," he snapped. "I don't want your pity. I've managed to take care of myself."

Francyne could see the hurt and anger that blazed in his eyes. She could feel the bitterness that emanated from him. This sudden withdrawal affected her deeply. Her pleasure ceased. She sat silently, pondering, with nothing to say, knowing that argument in a case like this was futile.

He saw her quandary, and he leaned over the table, his hand once again covering hers. He smiled apologetically. "I'm sorry, Francyne," he said gently. "I didn't mean to snap at you. I, like you, have strong feelings about marriage." His fingers lightly feathered over the top of her hand, tracing the contours of her bones. "I've seen the best relationships end with marriage."

"Maybe that's because the marriage partners don't work at making a success of their marriage," Francyne quietly remarked. "Marriage is like anything else—you get out of it what you put into it."

He laughed, genuinely amused now. "You're really an advocate of this outdated institution, aren't you?"

Francyne smiled, not the least perturbed by his criticism. "I am. I believe in it, and I want it for my life."

"I've seen affairs that are more permanent than most marriages," he commented dryly.

"Any relationship is as permanent as the commitment between the two partners," Francyne retorted authoritatively. "And one reason why a lot of marriages don't work is because the partners during their affair have thoroughly explored all the avenues of discovery, or so they think. Then when they finally get married, both of them slip into a boring routine. Love now becomes a chore; let's produce children. The courtship is a means to the end now—"

Brendan laughed, although the sound was gentle. "Now you're a marriage counselor!"

Francyne had the grace to blush and lower her head. She hadn't meant to get on her soapbox and regale him with her philosophy of love and marriage. Probably now she had completely severed any of the remaining strings that still held her and Brendan together.

"Sorry," she said. "I didn't mean to preach to you." She looked up and suddenly smiled, her eyes dancing with devilish delight. "I believe everything I said, but I shouldn't have inundated you with all my personal theories."

"Maybe I needed that little sermon," Brendan said, his voice low and intimate, again caressing her. "Perhaps I have been a little hasty in my condemnation." His brown eyes were warm and suggestive; his hands were assaulting the nerve endings in her palms, on her wrist.

He could see the drugged languor that was slowly glazing her eyes, and he could feel the increase in her pulse beat. With practiced expertise, with deliberate guile, he began to speak to her, telling her the lie that he had perfected through the years. The lie that slipped so easily from his lips. The lie that left no bitter taste in his mouth. The lie that didn't trouble his conscience.

"You've made me realize that I need to reconsider. Until today—" He left the sentence hanging, implying with his silence, reinforcing with his hands, stamping with the hot, branding touch of his eyes. "Until today I had never considered marriage."

Francyne colored prettily, and she lowered her eyes under his heated, penetrating gaze. Her blood clamored

53

through her veins, demanding its freedom. She fought to keep her breathing normal. She believed him.

Why shouldn't she believe me? he thought, altogether pleased with this turn of events. He had spent years perfecting these words. The right inflection, the softness, that wistful note of gratitude.

"What about children?" Francyne questioned softly, her face still suffused with a faint color. "Do you want children?"

He smiled, not willing to incur her displeasure again. "Let's just settle for my considering marriage today. We'll work on the children later." He grinned, lifting his eyebrows in a seductive gesture.

Francyne forced herself to laugh, then turned her face from him to look at the people who were walking by. In particular she watched a small child who was busily slurping his ice-cream cone. Brendan's words had both hurt and puzzled her. She realized with dismay that she was deeply affected by his declaration. She was too strongly attracted to him. Much too strongly! Her only defense was to affect indifference.

She kept watching the child, not wanting Brendan to see the conflict in her eyes, not wanting him to see the struggle within herself. God only knows, she thought, I'm old enough and wise enough to take care of my feelings. I'm certainly not going to wear them on my sleeve for him and the world to see. She would bide her time, play the game slowly and cautiously, and perhaps she would win! Perhaps!

"What are you thinking such deep thoughts about?" Brendan asked.

Francyne withdrew her hands from his grasp and grinned. "I was just thinking about what I would like to do."

His eyes lit up. "What?"

She lowered her voice until it was husky with seduction. "Let's go get an ice-cream cone."

At first his face was blank, then it was filled with surprise and incredulity. He leaned back in his chair and seriously surveyed the woman sitting across from him. Man, he thought with a slight twinge of anger, she had really let the wind out of his sails! And he still found her completely baffling.

Maybe she didn't care if he really would consider marrying her or not. Maybe she didn't care about him, period! If she did, she certainly didn't show it. All she was thinking about was a stupid ice-cream cone. What kind of woman was she, anyway? The question, the perplexity, clouded his eyes, furrowed his brow.

Francyne smiled. Again without being aware of it, he had allowed her to read his thoughts, and she enjoyed his discomfort. Let's see who can manipulate whom, she thought.

"Can we?" Again the soft, whispy pleading.

He laughed. "Why not? If that's what you want." He stood up, holding his hand out to her. "Lead the way."

Slowly they ambled to the bridge, crossed over, and walked up the familiar pathway until they reached the steep flight of stairs that carried them to the ice-cream parlor. After they had made their selection and had eaten their ice cream, they returned to the river, meandering up the walkway through the flurry of lights and activity into a quieter, more secluded area.

By tacit mutual consent, they stopped walking after a while and stood on the grassy bank of the river where Francyne leaned against the trunk of a tree. She sniffed deeply, keenly attuned to the sounds, the smell, the feel of the river and its vegetation. The gnarled tree, old and majestic, spread its boughs around them and swayed in the evening breeze, shining silver from the soft city light that filtered down to the river below. From where she stood she could see the shadowy outline of Brendan's profile. Then she turned to look at the river.

"I love this place," she breathed, inhaling the fragrance, looking at the river kingdom. "It's beautiful." She moved closer to the water, looking into its mirrored surface. "Don't you think it's beautiful?" she asked, looking at the reflection of the lights in its rippling surface.

She waited for his answer, but when it didn't come, she twirled around to see if he were still standing there.

"Do—" She softly asked again but didn't finish her question because she fell against the hardness of his chest.

His hands automatically came up to catch her, to keep her from losing her balance. But he didn't automatically release her; his hands kept clutching her shoulders, and he kept looking into her face, which was illuminated by the soft evening light.

"Oh," she mumbled, her heart racing, the palpitations loud enough for him to hear, she figured. "I . . . I . . . "

"Don't," he instructed her quietly, pressing a finger against her mouth. "Don't ruin it." He sighed, looking into her face, watching her hair as it softly wisped around her face, fanned by the breeze. "I agree. This is beautiful."

"I was talking about the river," she countered softly, smiling into his face, not perturbed that he was still holding her. She basked in the warmth of his embrace. She liked the feel of his tall leanness against her, and she breathed deeply—his after-shave lotion, the musky odor of his bath soap, all blending with that wondrous aura of the river, adding to its enchantment.

"I'm talking about you," he returned, his hands flexing over the softness of her upper arms.

Mesmerized, Francyne stared into the face that hovered so close to hers. She studied the ardent warmth that permeated those brown eyes, now discernible in the dim light; she looked at the amorous promise that spiraled out into the soft darkness. Her eyes flitted over the sensuous lips that were parted, curved into a smile. All her senses were alive and alerted to the man holding her. All her resistance was devastated by his nearness.

Brendan's lips lowered, and he murmured, "I didn't plan this, believe me, but I'd never forgive myself if I didn't take advantage of it. And you'd never forgive me either."

"What do you mean?" Francyne asked softly, her body swaying closer to his. She coyly batted her thick lashes, acutely aware of his height, his breadth. His nearness sent sharp spindles of desire splintering through her body.

"I'm going to kiss you."

The statement was soft, and his hands on her shoulders drew her closer to him. One hand carefully caught her glasses, pulling them from her face, dropping them into one of the compartments of the tote bag. Then he slowly brought her into his arms, giving her every opportunity to stop him. But Francyne, immobilized by the sheer magnetism of his presence, wouldn't have pulled back at this moment to save her life. She wanted the kisses of this man. She wanted to be loved by this man.

The warmth of his body infused her with euphoric abandon, the clean, fresh scent of him blending with the perfume of the flowers, drugging her with its ambrosial fragrance. One arm came around her waist, and strong fingers clamped around her neck, weaving themselves into the golden-brown mane that flowed down her back.

He drew her to him, placing her mouth exactly where he wanted it, and she willingly allowed him to do so. Her eyelids fanned against her cheeks, forming a sooty crescent on her tanned face. His head bent over hers, and she felt his warm, tingling mouth cover her own softly parted lips in a light, gentle kiss.

Then when she melded herself to him, altogether malleable and pliant in his arms, willingly kissing him with all her heart, trusting herself utterly to him and his passion, his kiss began to deepen. His mouth began to move on hers, opening wider, his tongue entering her mouth, wanting to drink the honey-sweet nectar.

Her mouth opened, welcoming the pillaging and plundering. She delighted in the feel of his hands as they gently kneaded the base of her neck, the fingers as they enveloped her waist, moving up and down her spine, sending thrills throughout her body in a thousand places at once. This was the beginning of ultimate intimacy, she thought hazily, her mental faculties not yet obstructed by the fog of passion. This is what she'd been searching for.

She and Brendan were made for each other. Their bodies fit together perfectly, as if some greater being had created them just for each other. Surely, she thought, fate had brought them together. Surely this was love! With this sweet thought racing through her mind, she moved, folding herself into that hard, sinewy body.

"Francyne," he breathed. "Oh, Francyne, if you don't stop that, I'm afraid that I won't stop."

"Yes, sir," she replied meekly, her lips tingling from the probing of his, her eyes glowing, stars of happiness in them.

She focused on the tiny gold chain that circled his neck. One of her hands moved from his shoulders, and her fingers traced the circle around his neck. Daringly she put her lips where her fingers had been, feathering light and breathy kisses around the same path that her fingers had blazed.

With an astonished expletive he gathered her to him, shudders running through his body as his lips came down to capture hers again. He gorged himself on the assenting sweetness of her mouth. Both of them reeled from the heady sensations they were experiencing in their discovery of each other. River Walk faded into obscurity around them as they teetered first, then fell over the brink into that bottomless abyss of joy that comes from having found that special someone.

When he finally released her, she clung to him, her fingers entwined in the thick curls behind his neck. She wouldn't have done this ordinarily, she mused, but Brendan was special . . . very special, and she didn't object. She was at peace with the world, caught up in the magic of the river. Nothing, nobody, mattered but her and Brendan. For the moment she had forgotten his cynicism and skepticism. Only joy at having found him coursed through her body, pounded in her bloodstream, gave life to her.

He guided her over to one of the benches, where they sat down. She was trembling after this onslaught of emotion, and he held her closely in his arms. "Are you cold?" His mouth caressed her ear, his breath blowing against her flushed cheeks.

"No," she whispered, "I'm not cold." She snuggled up to him, and they sat together, unconscious of the passing time, happy and complete in their silence, in each other. Finally, however, she pushed herself away.

"I've got to go," she announced reluctantly. She looked at her watch. "It's getting late."

He leaned down and picked up her tote bag and handed it to her. "I don't want you to leave, but since I have a sneaky feeling that you're not going to come up to my suite and look at my etchings, I'll walk you to your car."

Francyne chuckled. "Some other time perhaps."

Slowly and dreamily they made their way toward the hotel, to her car, walking no faster than they had on the way up. When he had tucked her behind the steering wheel, he shut the door and watched as she inserted the key in the ignition. She leaned against the back of the seat and stared into his face, wishing the evening didn't have to end. She was in no hurry to leave. She spoke first.

"I'll see you in the morning?"

"I thought you'd never ask," he breathed softly.

"About nine," she whispered, wondering if he was about to kiss her or not, watching his face as it drew closer, blocking out the city lights.

"About nine," he murmured, his mouth moving against hers with a light warmth, at first. Then he began to nibble, his teeth nipping the fullness of her lips. She clasped her hand around his neck and pressed his face against hers. Simultaneously her mind rebelled and her heart responded to the sensual assault. Still he didn't take her lips in a full kiss. Rather his tongue seductively traced the outline of her mouth, wringing an incoherent cry from her. His fingers closed around her neck, and his lips began to linger on hers in a fulfilling kiss, thankfully tasting, wanting more than this small sample, determined to have more. When her lips moved against his, he sensed the naked vulnerability of her soul.

"Oh, Brendan," she cried when she could speak. Her

stomach was turning somersaults. A fire was burning, the waves of heat blowing over her, suffocating her.

"Stay with me, Francyne," his lips whispered against hers.

"I can't," she returned softly, wrenching herself away from the touch of him, the taste of him, the smell of him. "I'm . . . I'm not like that."

Call me old-fashioned if you want to, she shouted silently, but that's what I am. "Sex has got to mean more than going to bed with someone." Her eyes were clear and lucid, her tone firm, no hint of apology in it. "When I go to bed with a man, it's because I love him."

He nodded. "Okay, Francyne." She could hear the coolness; she could see the difference in his face. "We'll play this your way."

With great effort he levered himself away from the car and smiled tightly at her, regretting that he respected her silly scruples. Respected them enough to keep himself from attempting to manipulate her into spending the night with him. He wondered what had happened to the Brendan O'Shea he knew so well.

He flexed his shoulders, trying to ease some of the strain out of his body. He knew that, given time, he could seduce her. He knew that given time with any other woman he probably would have seduced her. Yet this time he willingly stepped back, deferring his desires for the sake of her wishes. This was a first for Brendan O'Shea! It puzzled as well as angered him.

The engine turned over and purred to life.

"See you in the morning at nine." Her voice was low and husky; her lips were red and full, showing evidence of having been thoroughly kissed.

He nodded his head and stood watching as the car sped away, blending into the traffic of the still busy street.

CHAPTER THREE

"How do you like the Hanging Gardens?" Francyne asked, walking to the edge of the observation deck, a striking figure in her beige-eyelet-embroidered blouse and her dark brown walking shorts. She had a straw purse slung over her shoulder and clutched a plastic glass full of Coke in one hand.

"It's the best part of Aquarena," Brendan answered succinctly, refusing to let her lead him astray. "Now back to the question at hand," he enjoined briskly, his tone assuring her that he hadn't forgotten and that he wouldn't be deterred. He wanted an answer.

Pretending to be deeply enthralled by the view, she didn't turn to face him; she was standing with her back to him, her face toward the river. It would be a little while before she could answer him. Not because she was ashamed—perhaps a little bit disconcerted, but certainly not ashamed. She could understand why her mother and dad would come. But would he?

She half-turned, still not presenting a full view of herself. Nor could she see Brendan. Tenaciously she clutched the plastic container as if it were a life buoy and she were lost in the ocean with no hope of being found again. In short she wasn't paying too much attention to what was going on around her.

She didn't see the green material of Brendan's shirt as it stretched tautly against the muscles of his massive chest when he sat down on the bench directly behind her, carelessly leaning his elbows and back against the table. Nor did she see the bronzed skin at the vee of his shirt where the gold chain glistened in the sunlight. Because she wasn't looking, he allowed an arrogant smile to hover at the corner of his mouth, and he let his amusement overtly glimmer in his brown eyes.

"It wasn't a coincidence, was it?"

He knew the answer before he voiced the question, but he wanted to hear the admission from Francyne's own lips. When Keeley had suddenly presented them with the good news, he'd been surprised, but not too surprised to observe Francyne's reaction too.

Jumping up and down, Keeley had pointed to the entrance of the springs. "Look, Franny! There's Granny and Grampa."

Surprised! Yes, he admitted silently, he'd been surprised, and he'd spared Francyne a glance to see if she was as surprised as he. Evidently she wasn't. Her expression was simply pleased and expectant as her lips curved into a welcoming smile. She just waved and motioned for them to join her.

The LaRues' arrival didn't sit too well with Brendan. His affairs in the past hadn't included the parents, and he wasn't sure that he was ready for them now. He had bargained on Keeley's presence, but certainly not the mother and father. He watched through narrowed eyes as the couple approached them; he watched Francyne.

As they drew near Francyne turned to Brendan.

63

"Mom and Dad, this is Brendan O'Shea. Brendan, I'd like you to meet my parents, Sylvia and John LaRue."

Brendan had taken the hand that John offered and had smiled through the introduction. Naturally well versed in the niceties of etiquette, he said all the right things at the right time, but he wasn't pleased by their untimely arrival. A family reunion was just a little too much!

Sylvia, dressed in a pair of slacks with a matching floral blouse, had raked her hand through her short brown hair, laughing.

"We just happened to be passing by," she said, her face creasing into a generous smile. "We're on our way to Austin."

I'll bet, Brendan had seethed to himself, never letting the anger show in his eyes, keeping up that social front that called for a smile. Instead he had quipped sardonically, "What a coincidence!" His lips then formed the pasty smile. "So glad you could join us."

John LaRue chuckled softly and winked at his wife. "Seems to me like you've met your match, honey. I'll bet he thinks we're here to spend the day."

Sylvia's deep blue eyes sparkled mischievously. "Well," she droned slowly, enjoying Brendan's discomfiture, "it certainly does look like it, doesn't it?"

Francyne didn't really know what to do. True, she hadn't been surprised to see her mother. She knew Sylvia LaRue was a creature of impulse who gave in readily to her whims. And since she'd talked with Sylvia last night and had told her that she was bringing Brendan to the springs with her and Keeley, she had not been surprised to see them. Like a mother hen, Sylvia protected her little brood, and she wanted to meet the man Francyne was seeing.

Yet Francyne could imagine the thoughts that were

whirling through Brendan's head, and she was a little apprehensive. She remembered his cynical observations about love and marriage from last night, and she could imagine what he was thinking about the untimely arrival of her parents. Naturally because she loved them, she understood their concern and their curiosity, and she could afford to be lenient with them.

Without another word John turned in the direction of the restaurant, wiping the perspiration from his forehead. "Let's go to the bar and have a cold drink," he suggested. "I've never been one of these people who loves baking alive in the sun."

Brendan shrugged. "Sounds fine to me," he said unenthusiastically, wondering what he had gotten himself into. Not being a family person himself, he didn't find the situation even tolerable, much less enjoyable. Lagging behind, he followed them into the dimly lighted room.

Aware of Brendan's irritation at her parents' arrival, Francyne slowed her pace until she was walking beside him. She knew he was displeased, but there was nothing she could do about it now. Knowing her parents as well as she did, she imagined they had come to get Keeley, not to spend the day with them, but she couldn't say this to him at the moment.

By the time they had all seated themselves at the table, John was already at the bar ordering their drinks. Brendan had insisted on picking up the tab, but John refused.

"This is my treat, my boy. Both of us are so glad that Francyne isn't here with that Sterling what's-his-name that it's worth a round of drinks." Then he winked at Brendan and picked up the tray with their drinks, walking to the table. "Iced tea for Keeley and Granny, a strawberry daiquiri for Francyne, and two beers for the men." He held his up. "This is mighty cool and refreshing." He grinned at Brendan. "I'm afraid that you'll find this is the best part of the trip."

Francyne grimaced. "Oh, Dad!" and John's resonant laughter filled the small room.

Keeley giggled. "You always say that, Grampa." Suddenly she thought of something, and she lapsed into a spasm of giggles. She tugged Sylvia's arm. "Granny, do you remember last year when Sterling came, and he—"

Keeley didn't finish her sentence before Sylvia and John exchanged the sort of smug look that sometimes passes between husbands and wives when each knows what the other is thinking. They nodded their heads and began to laugh with Keeley. Francyne's laughter was slower in coming, and it was weaker.

Finally she could stand it no longer. "Hush," she warned them with embarrassment. "Don't make fun of him."

"What was his name?" John mused teasingly, running his finger absently over his top lip. "Let's see, Momma." He looked at Sylvia, his gray eyes frolicking with mischief. "Was it Sterling Bear or Sterling Bore?" A pause. "Of course—" He snapped his fingers. "It was Sterling Blair. Why can't I remember that?"

"Hush, Daddy," Francyne hissed in an undertone, trying not to laugh herself.

Keeley, jumping up and down in her chair, cried out, "You said he was Sterling Bore to begin with, Grampa, and then later he turned into Sterling Bear." She giggled, sipped her iced tea, then added, "You said all he could do was complain and growl."

Not wanting to leave Brendan in the dark, the three of them recounted that particular episode—and more —to Brendan, who sat back and listened with amusement. He especially enjoyed watching Francyne's features tighten with disapproval as her parents and Keeley talked and laughed about the incident.

After all the tales had been told and the laughter had subsided, Sylvia glanced at Francyne and saw the frown on her face. With parental intuition she knew that she had carried the joke a little too far in front of Brendan.

"Don't mind us," she apologized to Brendan, wiping the tears from the corner of her eyes. "We enjoy teasing Francyne, and we get carried away. Sterling's really a fine young man and not as bad as we picture him." She smiled placatingly at Francyne, who halfheartedly smiled back. Sylvia turned back toward Brendan. "But we are glad to have this chance to meet you, Brendan. It's time Francyne broke out of that shell she's been in. It's time she had more boyfriends."

Brendan chuckled and glanced at Francyne, enjoying the color, the deep red, that was mounting slowly from her throat to her cheeks to her forehead. And while Sylvia's attention was drawn to something Keeley was pointing at and John was busy buying himself another beer, Brendan leaned over to whisper into Francyne's ear.

"Are you glad that I'm the one who came with you?" Francyne just glared at him, twirling her straw around in the tall, cylindrical glass. "Tell me," he goaded, "which one is he? A bore, or a bear?"

Francyne hissed her answer under her breath. "Shut up, Brendan." She wished fervently that her mother would quit playing Cupid. For goodness sake, she was a grown woman!

Now her parents were gone, taking Keeley with them, leaving her and Brendan alone for the remainder of the day. Having seen the water show with Keeley, they were now strolling through the Hanging Gardens. Since her parents' departure she and Brendan had done little talking. She had pointed out several things, but he appeared to be deep in thought. Finally Francyne herself had lapsed into silence, enjoying the coolness of the wooded area. When Brendan suddenly voiced his question, it had taken her by surprise.

Brendan, pushing his elbows back a little more, squirming on the bench, was contented to watch Francyne, wondering at the thoughts that crowded her mind. He loved the sweet taste of victory, and he gloried in his ability to manipulate and ultimately dominate the opposite sex. At the moment he was luxuriating in his ability to influence one particular member of that sex. He was pleased that she had contrived at their being alone today. He was delighted that she wanted to be alone with him.

He watched her fingers flex around the cup, first squeezing, then relaxing, and he wondered if she was nervous or if it was just a habit. Whichever, he surmised with a superior smile, she was uncomfortable, probably mulling over her answer.

"Well?"

Francyne was glad that her back was turned to Brendan, and she was glad that her eyes were safely concealed by her sunglasses. She wouldn't let either his question or his assumptions intimidate her. In no hurry to confirm what he already supposed, she looked into the plastic cup at the caramel-colored liquid.

Because she was basically an honest person, she would tell him the truth, she would answer his question, and she would give him the satisfaction of hearing a verbal confession. But, she gloated openly, her lips curving into a full smile, she wouldn't give him the added pleasure of reading it in her eyes and on her face.

"Was it coincidental?" His voice demanded an immediate answer.

Francyne shook her head, still not looking at him. Her voice was low, so low that he could hardly hear, but her answer was steady and direct.

"No."

She felt the probing intensity of his gaze on her back, but she still didn't turn to face him. She knew what he was asking as surely as if he had expressed his thoughts aloud. He wanted an explanation. Again she spoke, her finger idly tracing the ridge around the rim of the glass.

"I called Mom last night, and when she and Dad found out that Keeley and I were coming here today, they decided to stop and meet us on their way to Austin." Abruptly she turned and looked squarely into his face, daring him to contradict her, daring him to question her further.

To meet *me*, Brendan silently corrected; his eyes spoke volumes, but his lips were sealed. Wisely he obeyed that I-dare-you-to-say-something look in Francyne's eyes. He grinned, but he remained silent.

Francyne walked to the table, swung her slender legs over the bench and sat down, still defying him to say a word. She knew to expect almost anything from her family, but today had really been a fiasco. What Sylvia and John hadn't told Brendan, Keeley had readily supplied, so that Francyne decided that she wasn't going to add to the saga. Probably the only tidbit of information that he didn't have was the answer to this one question. And it wasn't any of his business! She didn't propose to tell him why her mother and dad had come. It was enough that they had. He didn't need the double satisfaction of knowing that they were playing matchmaker.

Brendan's brown eyes never left her body. Each

movement intrigued him. As he waited patiently for her to continue her story a small, smirky gloat tugged at the corners of his mouth, and his eyes ran over her body, shutting out the beauty around him to concentrate totally on her. He watched her fingers as they fluttered from her collar to her small gold earrings. He saw the vagrant curl that fanned her cheek and would have reached out to tuck it behind her ear, but she anticipated him.

Her composure fully regained, she smiled at him; then she lifted the glass and sipped her Coke. When she set the glass on the table, he surmised—and rightly so—that she didn't intend to say any more on the subject. He frowned with displeasure and cocked his eyebrow.

"Just no?"

Francyne grinned and a soft laugh escaped her slightly parted lips. She lifted the glass again, not really wanting another swallow but wanting to hide her smile of triumph from him. She let the rim of the glass rest on her bottom lip.

She murmured with a faint huskiness, "Just no!" She volunteered no more information.

Brendan moved, swinging one leg over the bench, straddling it to face her. He scooted closer to her and, as was getting to be a habit, he captured her free hand in his and rubbed it softly, sending prickles of pleasure shooting through her veins.

"I'm glad they came," he said, his voice gruffly seductive, captivating its prey with its quiet confidence, lulling her into a languorous sense of sensual pleasure. He chuckled in that same quiet tone. "Not that I don't like Keeley, but I enjoy being with you."

Mesmerized, Francyne set her cup down but didn't break eye contact. She watched his fingers as they traced the invisible designs on her hand; she felt the heated excitement and desire that welled up inside her, flooding over her body, suffusing her with an acute, almost painful awareness of his powerful masculinity.

"I want to discover all of you." His voice was seductively arousing emotions that she—to give her credit—was trying desperately to quell, to control. With all the strength she could muster, she tore her eyes from those fingers. She stared into her cup, which was almost empty now.

Get hold of yourself, she admonished sharply, never thinking about pulling her hand from his grasp. He knows what he's doing. Can't you tell? He's an expert when it comes to seducing women, and remember, you're just one of many. Look what he's done to you in less than two days! Think what will happen in two more!

She inhaled deeply, lifted her face, and looked at him, smiling. "Keeley's quite a handful," she commented, deliberately straying from the subject. "If you're around her much, you'll find out that she's the family chatterbox."

And don't believe everything that she says, Brendan silently added, following her train of thought only too well. He returned her smile, the golden flecks in the rich brown of his eyes mocking her. You don't fool me, he announced to himself, but she read his eyes.

"Umhumm," he droned soothingly, the musical tones velvet-smooth to Francyne's ragged nerves, "but she can be a source of much valuable information."

Francyne flushed, remembering every bit of pertinent information that Keeley had blurted out to him. At the time she had laughed it off, hoping that Brendan would do the same, hoping that perhaps he hadn't been paying too close attention.

"She's just a child," Francyne went on, with a slight shrug. "She often calls things as she sees them, not as they really are."

Brendan chuckled, his husky voice thick with amusement. "Ah, Francyne," he chided, his hand moving to her chin, his thumb stroking the soft silkiness of her lower lip.

Slowly he leaned forward, his lips gently seeking and finding the sensitive earlobes. His voice dropped to a whisper that blew tantalizingly into her ear, sending thrills to all her nerve endings, passion bumps rising on her arms.

"Don't tell me that Keeley imagined all those nice things that you said about me!"

His teeth gently nipped her earlobes; his hands gently feathered trails of wild fire over her hands; he deliberately seduced all her senses. His voice thickened with his growing desire, the throaty sound contributing to Francyne's emotional turmoil.

"I rather enjoyed hearing them."

Shaken by his voice, devastated by his touch, Francyne moved only her lips. "Perhaps Keeley didn't imagine them," she admitted, "but maybe I didn't say them. Maybe Keeley said them."

His mouth brushed up the side of her face, nipping its way from her ear to the corner of her mouth. "Maybe Keeley said them, but you must have agreed."

Her voice was breathlessly still. "Keeley talks so much that I answer most of the time without even hearing what she says."

"That, lady," Brendan whispered, his lips hovering above hers, his breath—still smelling like Coke—fanning the wisps of hair at her temples, "can get you into a lot of trouble."

His hands now clasped her shoulders, and with no

effort on his part and no resistance on hers, he pulled her toward him. She closed her eyes in anticipation of the sexual onslaught. Instead she felt the whisper-soft touch of his thumbs as they moved tormentingly over her shoulders, circling slowly as if he were memorizing the feel of her silky skin. The total effect was so hypnotic that she started to sway toward him, never thinking that someone might come upon them at any moment, and not caring what they would think if they did come.

As if he had read her thoughts, Brendan chuckled softly, and instead of taking the proffered gift of her honeyed mouth, instead of ravishing those full red lips that pouted for his kiss, his lips, feather-light, brushed her closed eyelids, her flushed cheeks, and the corner of her mouth.

"Do you mean to say," he demanded in that low, gravelly voice, "that you didn't say I was a 'hunk'?"

Francyne laughed, intoxicated by his nearness, drugged by his caresses. She drew a deep, ragged breath, hoping to break away from her captor, hoping to escape this sensual trap. Instead she swayed toward the man whose lips she wanted, whose touch she invited.

"Maybe I did say that," she said carelessly, thrilling to the welcomed touch, turning her mouth, seeking for the fullness of his, wanting to put an end to this maddening torment.

She wanted the knot in her stomach untied; she wanted the racing pulses stopped; she wanted the amorous drumbeat of her heart to be stilled. Never had she felt such compelling emotions; never had reason been so easily cast aside.

The golden sound of her laughter floated toward him, and desire surged through his body, into his loins, making him potently aware of her. He wanted her with

73

a primitive longing that was closely akin to lust. The weight of her breasts pressing against his chest didn't help him to restrain his desire, nor did the hardening of her nipples as she wriggled closer to him.

She was oblivious to her surroundings, but he had heard people coming, their loud voices and laughter. He had to bring her back to the present; he had to jolt her down from that erotic cloud on which she was floating. Also, he reluctantly admitted, he had to pull himself together.

His mouth moved on the corner of hers when he spoke. "One thing about making love with your eyes closed," he teased softly, "is that you never know when someone's going to walk up on you unawares."

Francyne's eyes flew open, and she looked around guiltily, her face flushing crimson. Hurriedly, clumsily she pressed her hands to his chest and pushed herself away, raking her fingers frantically through her hair, twiddling with the collar of her blouse, stroking the small gold earring in the lobe of her left ear. Nervously she bit her lower lip, looking into Brendan's eyes, almost drowning in the tender laughter that swirled in their depths.

"How—how did you know that my eyes were closed?" she asked, her fingers tentatively touching her sunglasses, which were slightly askew.

"You let me get close enough to see through them."

Aware of what he was doing and ready to suffer the consequences, Brendan reached out and gently grasped the nosepiece of her glasses between his thumb and index finger and pulled them off. She blinked several times as her eyes grew accustomed to the light, but she said nothing. However, she did lower her lashes in an attempt to hide the passion that still flamed there.

His hand balled into a fist, and he tapped her chin,

lifting her face. His voice, once again, had dropped until it was nothing more than a whisper on the soft breeze that wafted through the wooded paradise.

"I think you're a foxy lady." He loved that look of shy innocence that spread across her face. He spoke softly. "It's no shame to let your needs show in your face or in your eyes. A man likes to know that he's wanted too. Contrary to popular opinion, he doesn't want to fight the woman every time he makes love." He smiled, so gently, so tenderly, that Francyne couldn't think beyond the moment, beyond his words, beyond his touch.

She blushed, licking her lower lip, glazing it with a shining nectar that seemed to compel the touch of his lips. Still she didn't raise her lashes, wishing she had something to hide behind, not knowing that Brendan was fighting the same wild, riotous emotions, that he was using all his willpower to control his needs and desires.

She did know, however, that it was too early in their friendship . . . affair . . . for her to reveal too much of herself to him. She wasn't ready to be hurt, and she wasn't sure that she could continue to see him without being hurt. She knew exactly how he felt about love and commitment, and she knew that she would accept nothing less. She was also aware that as long as she kept her lashes lowered, hiding her eyes behind the sooty crescent curtain, Brendan wouldn't know that she was spinning in a whirlpool of chaotic and conflicting thoughts.

How could he do this to her? she asked herself. He was almost a stranger, yet she felt she had known him longer than anyone else. Not just a man, she corrected herself hazily, allowing her thoughts to ascend to that cloudy reef of fantasy, willingly giving in to this recurrence of desire. He was like a lover. *A lover.*

That thought alone jarred her out of her reverie of sensual abandon. Quickly she plucked her glasses from Brendan's unresisting fingers and crammed them on her face, having to adjust them several times because of her nervousness. Disconcerted because Brendan was laughing at her, she lifted the long-forgotten cup of Coke, sipping at the warm, flat-tasting liquid.

Then with quick, jerky movements she stood up and walked to the edge of the deck, dropping her cup into the litter barrel. Rather than returning to the bench, however, she stayed where she was, looking down at the river.

"We'd better go," she announced in a small pristine voice, which added to Brendan's amusement.

He smiled, but did not answer. He was enjoying her pose of injured innocence, and he was willing to let her revel in it for a while. He was willing to play follow-the-leader, as long as Francyne was the leader. Yes, he thought, swinging his leg over the bench, his smile broadening, his brown eyes twinkling with amusement, he would let her think she was the leader for a little longer.

"Whatever you say" was his quiet comment as he stood up, crumpled his cup and tossed it into the barrel, then followed her across the wooden platform and up the steps to the curio shop.

Afterwards they slowly ambled down the narrow, paved pathways through the dense South Texas forest that matted the hillside. The trees, rugged and gnarled, grew low to the ground with spreading branches, and in such profusion that they formed a green canopy over the winding trails. The intimate atmosphere inspired

Brendan to take Francyne's hand and to hold it as they alternately walked and loitered in the shade of the trees.

Finally they were standing in front of the gristmill, watching the old water wheel laboriously roll around, splashing water and groaning with each rotation. Brendan, standing slightly behind Francyne, put his hands on her shoulders, the heel of each hand softly kneading the flesh of her upper arm.

"Was Keeley just chattering when she said Sterling came over last night?"

Francyne could hear the grating displeasure in his voice.

"No." She couldn't be more direct.

"And you had an argument?" He was determined to learn more.

"Yes," Francyne replied in a low, steady voice, never taking her eyes from the water wheel. "We did."

"Want to tell me about it?" he asked, knowing without being told that he was the subject of their disagreement.

She shrugged. "There's nothing to tell. Sterling got mad, and we had a quarrel."

"He's angry because you're spending the day with me, isn't he?" His grasp tightened on her shoulders, and he pulled her pliant body closer to his. "You argued because he didn't want you to come here with me today?"

"Yes." Just that, nothing more.

Brendan had a stabbing pain in his belly that nearly ripped him to pieces. He hated the thought of Sterling's being at her apartment; he hated the thought of Sterling Blair being even a small part of Francyne's life. And he was angry because she had so lightly dismissed this argument, because she didn't want to confide in him.

77

She belonged to him—Brendan O'Shea—and she had no right to be with any other man.

"Did you know he was coming over?"

He strove to keep his voice even, but the thought that she had left him to go meet Sterling was driving him out of his mind. Ever since Keeley had told him about Sterling's visit, he had wanted to confront Francyne; he had wanted to demand an explanation. Yet his better judgment had warned him that a confrontation would destroy his chances of establishing a deeper, more meaningful relationship with her.

Francyne shook her head, still being honest with him. "No, he surprised me." She breathed deeply, exhaling slowly, remembering too well the heated exchanges of the night before. "I hadn't been home long before he came over." Brendan felt her body tense as she moved her shoulders slightly, perhaps in a shrug of some sort. "You know Keeley! She began to talk nonstop about your coming here with us, and Sterling hit the ceiling."

"I thought he was nothing more than a friend," he commented dryly, holding back the sarcasm.

The tender fondling of her shoulders continued, and the equally seductive tremor of his voice continued to play havoc with her nerves. She didn't resist the passionate feelings that slowly coursed through her body, beginning at her shoulders, radiating in all directions. She wanted the warmth of those hands all over her body.

Her stomach hurt; it ached with an insatiable want, her body asking for the welcome release of her emotions. Giving in to the floodtide of emotions, she turned her face, hunched one shoulder, and kissed the back of his hand, nuzzling it with her cheek.

"I thought so, too," she eventually admitted, trying

to ignore her growing desires, "but apparently not. He's jealous."

Brendan's chin brushed against the crown of silken hair that blew in the early evening breeze. "He's got every right to be jealous," he told her quietly. "I meant what I said yesterday."

Suddenly aware of a large crowd descending on the gristmill and the spring house, he dropped his hands from her shoulders, caught her hand in his, and led her up the short flight of stone steps behind the mill. When they reached a secluded corner, out of the main flow of traffic, he began to speak.

"I meant it, Francyne. I intend to take you away from Sterling. I'm going to be the only man in your life for a long time."

Not forever, she noted. Just for a long time.

His eyes shimmered with a lazy look of sensuous pleasure, soft and warm, but beneath that calm and serene surface lay the flinty bedrock of determination.

"I want you."

Not I love you, she thought.

So strong was the visual caress that Francyne almost forgot to breathe again, but his last three words . . . *I want you* . . . had the effect of a cold stream of water. He said the words as if that were all there was to it. *I want you.*

She shook her head. There was more than *I want you.*

"Want isn't good enough, Brendan. I've had enough of want to last me the rest of my life." Tears sparkled in her eyes, but he couldn't see them; her sunglasses protected her. "I've had enough men in my life who wanted. This time I'm settling for nothing less than love."

Her reply, much to his amazement, hurt him. He wasn't sure why, but it did. He was a man of the world, and experience through the years had been his teacher. He had gained expertise in the art of seduction, and he had never denied himself pleasure or fulfillment. Why should he expect her to be any different? After all she was nearly twenty-eight.

But he had wanted her to be different. God, just the thought of her going to bed with another man just to satisfy her needs and wants cut him deeply. He wanted her to be innocent; he wanted to believe that she had been waiting for him to come along to awaken those hidden flames of desire that smoldered in the deep recesses of her inner being.

His brown eyes pierced through the dark lenses, seeking an answer to his dilemma, seeking the truth in order to put his doubts to rest. She had seemed so guileless; she talked innocently; she felt innocent. Could his intuition be wrong? He didn't know. Did it matter? It shouldn't . . . but it did.

Francyne saw the question, the hurt, the puzzlement mirrored in his expressive eyes, but she didn't try to explain. This was neither the time nor the place. Their relationship hadn't reached the stage where she would pour out her secrets to him. Instead she defended Sterling.

"I like Sterling a lot, Brendan. He's been a good friend to me." She stared directly into his face. "It would take more than want—as you put it—to take me away from him."

Brendan's face registered surprise and clouded with displeasure. His voice sounded like thunder when he demanded contemptuously, "Why this sudden show of interest? Yesterday you didn't hesitate to let me know that you were just friendly."

Francyne, not able to stand the derision in his eyes, twisted out of his grasp and moved closer to the fence that crossed the pathway. "I wasn't serious," she admitted. "That is, I'd never thought about making a commitment to Sterling until last night." She faltered, as if uncertain whether to continue or not. "I . . . I didn't know how he felt about me. I didn't know that he loves me." She tried to laugh, but the sound was a bitter one. "I've . . . I've never seen him as more than a friend, but last night—" She paused. "I'd hurt him so much. I could hardly stand it."

Brendan, having suspected all along that Sterling regarded her as his exclusive property, marveled at her ignorance of such matters. He shook his head as if to put his disorganized thoughts into order. It was this naiveté that threw him off guard and perplexed him. He didn't know how to figure her. He lifted a hand, running it over the back of his head, letting his fingers rest on the nape of his neck.

"He proposed to you, didn't he?" He saw the curt nod. "What was your answer?"

With a haughty lift of her brow she retorted coolly, "I don't think you've a right to ask that question, much less get an answer." She breathed deeply, her breasts rising and falling beneath the cotton shirt. "Just because Momma and Daddy make fun of Sterling doesn't mean anything. Not to me, I make up my own mind about a man—with or without their approval." Her voice had risen in volume and intensity. "He . . . he loves me."

She waited to see what his comment would be.

Brendan hesitated, knowing that he had erred. Eventually he asked, "Do you—" A short pause. "Do you think that you love him?"

Although he was hesitant and cautious, Brendan was also relentless in his probing. He didn't care that he was getting personal, and there was barely suppressed rage behind every word. He asked the question using her terminology. *Love* wasn't a word that he included in his vocabulary. To him *love* was a word people used when they wanted a euphemism for "lust." It was a word that cowards hid behind when they didn't want to face reality.

For Brendan sex was no more than a pleasurable experience, especially if both he and his partner liked and respected one another, but certainly he'd never felt that part of him belonged to a woman, that part of her was his. And he'd certainly never met the woman yet who could ruin him for all other women. He'd never met one that he couldn't live without. To add a postscript—he hoped he never would.

Brendan repeated his question. "How do you feel about him?"

"I . . . I like him," she admitted. Brendan's silent anger forced her to continue. "He said I'd learn to love him, given time," she muttered. "He said he loves me enough for both of us."

Dear God! Brendan expostulated under his breath. I've never heard such hogwash in all my life!

He moved closer to her, catching her shoulders, jarring her against his taut body.

"I don't want to spoil Sterling's perfect little dream, but this man can't give you what you need, Francyne."

"He can't?" she asked in a cool, distant voice.

"He can't," Brendan grated between clenched teeth. She stared at him.

"You told me last night that when you went to bed with a man, there had to be more than sex." He snorted derisively. "Well, today I'm here to tell you that if you marry Sterling, feeling the way you do, you won't be sharing anything more than sex with him." His voice was hard and cold.

"You're horrid," Francyne gasped furiously, trying to jerk out of his tight grip. She was abashed at his ability to use her own argument against her.

"Not horrid," he negated, "just realistic."

"Well," Francyne replied helplessly, "you're too personal." She writhed but could not escape his arms.

"You're so right," he purred caustically. "I'm getting very personal. I don't want to see you marry, period, but if you do insist upon it, don't marry anyone out of pity." He pulled her into his arms, circling her with the protective warmth of his embrace. "Let me teach you all the intricacies of making love, Francyne. Let me awaken all that passion that burns somewhere deep inside you, that part of you that no man has touched before. Can't you feel the attraction between us? We're made for each other."

The scorching touch of his flesh brushing hers, the fiery warmth of his voice almost threw her into oblivion, separating her body from her mind. Yet she mustered the strength to keep her voice calm, to think reasonably straight.

"So you think we're made for each other," she asked.

"I do." There was no arrogance in his statement, just a simple, honest promise. "Will you give me a chance to prove it to you?"

Francyne was saved from answering when two small children scampered up the steps to join them. When they realized, however, that the path was a dead end, they skipped back down, but by now Francyne and Brendan had separated.

He reached for her hand, but she quickly followed the children down the steps. "I said," he repeated in a low voice, "will you give me a chance?"

She threw him an enigmatic glance over her shoulder. "We'll see." She was not obliged to listen to his response to this, because she was on the bottom step, headed for the spring house. She quickly pulled on the door and walked inside, welcoming the cool air-conditioning. She sat at one of the antique round tables and waited for Brendan's to appear.

When he did, he was scowling, but one glance around the room wiped the grimace from his face. His lips twitched into a broad smile. Looking at her, he said, "I know. Don't tell me. I'll never forget."

He walked to the ice-cream counter and was about to select the flavor when he glanced into the corner and saw the cheese block and the cracker barrel. He turned back to Francyne.

"Ice cream or cheese and crackers?"

"Cheese and crackers, this time." She smiled. "Not much."

She took her glasses off and put them on the table, letting him see her eyes, which were sparkling with sheer devilment. She suspected that he wasn't overly pleased with her dinner plans.

"I don't want to spoil my dinner. Mom always cooks a feast."

He simply chuckled, remembering how easily he had allowed Sylvia to wrap him around her little finger. He, a man who had never allowed himself to become intimately involved with anyone's family, not even his own, had quickly given in to Sylvia's persuasive charm. Before he realized it, he had accepted her invitation to stop by the lake house for dinner on their way home that evening. He smiled at Francyne. What wouldn't he do for this woman?

CHAPTER FOUR

The apartment was spotless, Francyne couldn't have looked more delightful, and the aroma of freshly perked coffee and banana bread wafted tantalizingly through the air. Nervously Francyne walked in front of the mirror for the umpteenth time, tugging on her blouse, retying the grosgrain ribbon that secured her ponytail, pirouetting to see if her white skort fit well enough.

She smiled, remembering the woman who had sold it to her. "Really, dear," she had explained with a wicked little grin, "it's a skort—a bouncy little short that has all the fullness of a skirt." She stood back, watching Francyne model it. "Just right for your tanned legs, dear. Very nice!" She looked at the orange loose-fitting blouse with the short-rolled sleeves and the white-contrast collar trim. "This is an excellent selection. The orange seems to do something to your eyes." She squinted, adjusted her glasses, and peered into Francyne's face. "They seem to be a golden topaz.

Most unusual color, dear." She shook her head. "Most unusual."

The short taps on the doorbell broke into her reverie, and she quickly moved across the thick-pile carpet, her designer tennis shoes hardly making a sound. She didn't have to wonder who the caller was. Brendan had promised last night when she dropped him at his hotel that he would spend the day with her, and they would begin by having breakfast at her place.

She opened the door wide, a dazzling smile curving her lips. Her eyes sparkled, and this time there were no sunglasses to cover them. For a long time he lingered over their beauty, amazed by their changeable hue. Somehow or another, he thought, they added a new and unsuspected dimension to her personality. Would he ever really know her? Or was she as elusive as her eyes?

"Good morning."

Just two words! A greeting everyone has heard a million times in their lives! Yet it turned Francyne's legs to jelly. She stared at the vibrant black curls that framed his face, the thick eyebrows that accented those warm brown eyes, which glowed with renewed promise. She looked at the fine laughter lines that dashed the corners of his eyes, and she licked her lips with healthy desire as she stared at his sensuous lips and even, white teeth.

Her eyes flowed downward, catching the glint of that small chain, and she wished that she were that fortunate. She wished she could burrow into that riot of dark hair, close to that bronzed body. She wanted to feel that pulse beat; she wanted to hear every thump of his heart. Shivering with the intensity of her thoughts, she forced her gaze on downward.

She took in the reddish-brown western shirt, the

three top buttons loose so that it veed, revealing his muscular chest, the sleeves cuffed so that his forearm was bared, covered with the same springy curls that matted his chest. Both hands rested on his hips, which were encased in a pair of expensive, though faded, jeans.

"If you're through taking in the view, ma'am," he teased softly, his tone mocking her Texas drawl, "I'd like to come in. Standing out in the hall staring at a beautiful woman in a pair of shorts isn't my idea of fun." The corners of his eyes crinkled, and his brown eyes darkened with laughter. "It can be rather hard on a fellow, if you know what I mean."

Francyne blushed a deep red at his double meaning and quickly jumped aside to let him into her apartment. She was so embarrassed that she could hardly mutter, "Come in." For a second or two she avoided direct eye contact and took an extra long time in closing the door. She needed to regain her composure before she could face him.

When she finally did turn, she bumped into him, because he hadn't moved from the foyer. Reaching one of his arms over her shoulder, he quickly secured the lock before he dropped both hands to her waist, clasping it tightly but tenderly, pulling her toward him. His lips lightly kissed her forehead, trailing a moist path to her lips.

He husked against her warm skin. "I could hardly wait for this morning." A pause. "I almost didn't wait."

Her hands, daring in their exploration, inched up his broad chest and locked around his neck, and she stood looking up into his face, her breasts cushioned against the hardness of his upper torso, her naked thighs brushing against the soft cotton of his jeans.

87

"I'm glad you came," she uttered, her voice low and caressing.

Again she radiated innocence, yet Brendan also sensed an undercurrent of maturity and experience. Again he was puzzled. The only certainty about her was the elusive beauty of her eyes and his growing desire to possess her, to know her fully, the physical, the intellectual, the spiritual. Nothing else seemed to matter; nothing else was important. He had to unravel the mystery called Francyne LaRue.

"I'm glad too."

Then his lips captured hers in that early morning kiss. A kiss that was deep and long, warm and intoxicating. A kiss that both of them wanted. A kiss that began with restraint, but as each melded himself to the other their fiery passion ignited to burn away all inhibitions, all restraints, all obstacles, all barriers. By mutual agreement the fire flared from the sputtering embers into an all-encompassing blaze. Both of them welcomed its searing heat. Both of them fanned the blaze until it was a wild inferno, flames dancing higher and higher, consuming everything in its path.

Her mouth opened to the thrusting demands of his tongue, and her tongue whispered and touched his, stroking, inviting, enticing. His hands slipped down, his fingers massaging softly as they traveled the length of her spine, stopping at the hips, where they fanned out. Just the feel of those hot fingers drew her closer to the desire that surged through him, the close contact leaving Francyne in no doubt as to the urgency of his needs. Not consciously aware of what she was doing but instinctively in touch with what her body wanted and needed, Francyne rubbed her hips against him, thrusting her softness against the hardness of his loins.

His deep gasp of pleasure sent the heated blood rushing through her veins, and she threw caution to the winds. She matched his kiss in ardor, her hands touched in equal measure, her legs pressed into the flexed muscles of his. She couldn't taste enough of him; she couldn't touch enough of him.

When he lifted his lips, he drew a ragged breath before he muttered, "This is the beginning of a delectable breakfast."

"Umhumm," she murmured huskily, her emotions soaring, speech denied her.

His firm, full lips, however, didn't stop their pilfering as he talked. They invaded, conquered, explored every nook and cranny; the captor arrogantly and confidently took the vanquished. In between delicious nibbles he murmured sweet nothings to her, and she murmured to him, both understanding the passionate babble.

Finally in a passion-thickened voice he said, "I've always been fond of breakfast in bed. Would you join me?"

Lost . . . willingly so . . . in the vortex of desire, Francyne rested her cheek on his chest, listening to the erratic beating of his heart, moving with his sporadic breathing. His invitation, one she shouldn't accept, sounded delicious, and she was hungry, hungry for the completion of his love.

When she didn't reply, he asked, "Which door?"

She tossed her head in the direction of her bedroom. "That one." He tugged at her, but she didn't follow. She shook her head. "We can't." A soft ringing sound in the kitchen punctuated her remark. "My timer," she explained in answer to Brendan's puzzled expression. "My banana bread's ready." She pulled out of his grasp and moved to the kitchen. "I don't want it to burn." She smiled. "I baked it especially for you."

Left standing in the middle of the living room, Brendan dumbfoundedly shook his head and gave a snort of disgust. He couldn't have cared less about banana bread. At the moment banana bread was the *least* of his desires. Drawing a deep breath or two, he followed her into the kitchen and watched as she concentrated on her baking. He stood in the door frame, leaning against one side, his arm propped up on the opposite side.

She set the hot pan on the counter and dropped the dishrags beside it. "Banana bread is a specialty in our family," she said wildly, sporadically talking to cover her embarrassment.

She had suddenly realized how nearly Brendan had come to seducing her, and the idea that she was an easy conquest filled her with burning shame. To say she was discomfited was an understatement. Dear Lord, she thought, he hadn't been in the apartment ten minutes before they were headed for the bedroom.

"Do you want it when it's hot or cold?" she asked, opening the cabinet above the counter and taking down her bread plate. "I always like it hot." She pulled on the drawer, extracted a knife, and cut the bread into thick slices. "I like to spread butter over it and eat it when it's still warm like this."

As she kept up a stream of nervous chatter Brendan went into the kitchen and sat down at the table. His lips parted in a crooked grin, and he wondered if she were aware of how completely flustered she sounded.

"I haven't eaten it before," he casually replied. "Fix me some the way you like it."

Francyne set the platter on the table and walked over to the refrigerator. "Do you want coffee or milk with yours?" She yanked on the door and pulled out the plastic carton.

"Coffee, please. Strong and black." He grinned and reached out to still one of her hands, which was fiddling nervously with the pleat in her skort. "Take it easy," he said gently. "Nothing happened."

She didn't reply, she just looked at him, glad of the interruption. If it hadn't been for the banana bread . . . She didn't dare think anymore about it. She set her glass of milk on the table, poured Brendan his cup of coffee, and sat across from him. She buttered two pieces of bread liberally, putting one on his plate, the other on hers.

Don't rush it, Brendan thought, sipping the hot coffee, picking up his slice of bread. You've got all day. And you know it's just a matter of time. She's jumpy. He took a large bite of the warm bread. Not bad! She's got to get used to the idea. At least it's been awhile for her. Pleasure spread through him in sweet waves. Her hesitancy thrilled him.

He finished his bread. "Not bad," he said appreciatively, picking up a second slice of bread, adding a generous slab of butter. "You bake this all the way?"

Francyne dimpled, nodding her head. "From scratch. Mom's a fantastic cook, and she taught both of us to cook from the time we were in the cradle." She chuckled, remembering Sylvia's incessant chatter as she scurried the girls around in the kitchen. "Mom always said that it was most important that we learn to cook." Her eyes took on a soft, dreamy look. "She said if we learned to cook that we'd be sure to—" *Get a husband!*

She stopped in the middle of her sentence and blushed, dropping her eyes to her plate. Taking her index finger, she began to brush the crumbs around the slick surface of the ceramic. She hadn't meant to say that, she thought with embarrassment. She knew how Brendan felt about marriage, and she didn't want to keep harping on it. God knew, that wasn't what she meant, but would he?

"You'd be sure to what?" Brendan prompted, fascinated with the paradoxical creature that was sitting across from him. At one point he would think he had her figured out; then again he would wonder at the complexity of her personality.

Francyne shrugged the subject away. "Nothing," she smiled, in an attempt at nonchalance. "Mom's always yakking, and I seem to have inherited that trait this morning." Her golden eyes, spinning with dark brown glints, smiled at him too. "I'm sorry that I've been behaving so childishly. I'm . . . I'm just not . . . not accustomed to . . . to . . . " She would make herself finish the sentence. " . . . entertaining men in my apartment . . ." Her voice dropped but she hadn't finished yet. ". . . like this."

A large hand stilled the movements of her smaller one, clasping it loosely in his. The dark brown eyes, hot and feverish in their intimacy, in their sincerity, probed into hers, piercing to her very soul.

Softly she caught the words "I'm glad you don't."

He said nothing more; they just sat quietly, savoring the presence of each other, Brendan plotting a new approach, Francyne wondering how long she could resist. Not long, she knew. As much as the thought titillated her senses, it filled her with apprehension. She couldn't help but associate her feelings for Brendan with getting hurt.

Gently she tugged her hand loose, lifted her glass, and drained the last drop of milk. "Would you care for any more bread or coffee?"

Brendan shook his head. "No, thanks." He put his empty cup on top of his plate. "Want any help cleaning up?"

Francyne pushed her chair back and stood up, lifting the platter of bread. "No, I'll just put the dishes in the dishwasher and the bread in the keeper."

Brendan nodded and walked into the living room to pull the drapes, looking over the large courtyard below, green and lush with trees and foliage. His first opportunity had been thwarted. Thus, he had to create another one. The timing had to be right, the atmosphere, the setting. It had to seem natural, not selfconscious or contrived.

I wonder, he thought, his fingers tugging at his lips. A few drinks. Swim. Relax. That might do it. It was surely worth a try. He heard the swish as the door closed behind her.

He pointed out the window. "Lovely view. Do you swim?"

She shook her head. "I putter around in the water, but I can't swim. How about you?"

He shrugged. "Good enough. Want to give it a try?"

She read the silent message.

"What about breakfast?" she stalled, knowing that she was losing ground. Brendan O'Shea had one purpose, and one purpose only. He fully intended to make love to her—with her willing consent.

He smiled, the gentle curve of the lips most seductive. "I'm not a heavy eater. The banana bread and coffee were fine." He saw her indecision. "After we've had our swim, I'll take you out for lunch."

She didn't answer; qualms and apprehension clouded her eyes.

"We'll have plenty of time. Your mom's not going to bring Keeley home until late this afternoon. We'll be back in time."

She wasn't worried about being home in time for Keeley's arrival. She was worried about herself. Could she survive an affair with this man? Did she want to live without trying?

He had to press her. Couldn't give her too much time to think. "Well?"

She nodded her head and smiled gingerly. "Okay." She didn't move. "What about your bathing suit?"

Brendan guffawed at the question. "Yes, Franny dear, I have a bathing suit with me. I only skinny-dip when I'm absolutely certain that I won't be disturbed." He moved toward the door. "I'm taking my things over to the apartment later today, and I have my suitcases in the car." He shrugged. "Simple as that."

Again she nodded, smiling tremulously at him, heading toward her bedroom. After she closed the door behind her, she slowly walked to the dresser, pulled out a drawer, and extracted a new swimsuit. With trembling fingers she unbuttoned her blouse, pulled it from the waistband of her skort, shrugged out of it, and tossed it on the chest at the foot of the bed. She unfastened the waistband of the skort and kicked out of it, throwing it on top of the blouse. Her bra and panties followed quickly.

She stepped into the bandeau maillot suit, black with richly colored gardenias bordering the top and streaking diagonally from the left down to the right. The adjustable legs would tie as high as she dared, but she didn't dare too much. Walking to the closet, she pulled out an ankle-length terry cloth poncho that had a drawstring at the waist.

She dropped it over her head, tied the drawstring, and slipped her feet into a pair of thongs. Now, she thought, looking at herself in the mirror, I feel safer, more secure.

Moving into the bathroom, she grabbed two large towels and returned to the living room to find Brendan

94

lounging on the sofa, looking absently out the window. She wasn't prepared for the sight of his nearly naked body.

When he heard the door close, he looked in her direction with ludicrous astonishment, and laughter, the sound rich, deep, and sonorous, rumbled from his chest. "Ah, Francyne!" he breathed when he finally could talk. "What am I going to do with you?" He stood up, walking toward her. "First, you decline my offer of breakfast in bed, and now"—his hand swept down the length of her body—"you deny me the pleasure of seeing your body."

Francyne laughed, exhilarated by the knowledge that she excited Brendan, and that he was not very taken with her all-concealing poncho. She couldn't quite understand this change in her personality, but Brendan had brought it about. Before he came into her life, she had kept her relationships on a friendly basis. She had soon learned that most men were governed by their need and desires, with no thought for the woman's. How many times she'd been hurt and disillusioned.

But with no doubt in her mind Francyne knew that when the right time came . . . and it would . . . she would give herself to Brendan with no holds barred. She would welcome more than just these preliminary advances. She would insist on giving herself to him entirely.

Never in her life had she felt this way, but with Brendan she felt her emotions surge through her veins and race through her heart, carrying the airy sensation to her brain. She felt that sensuous abandon that compels one person to become an intimate part of another in the ceremony of love. And there was no doubt in her mind that it was love . . . at least for her.

All the time that these tumultuous thoughts were clamoring in her mind, her eyes raked over the majestic figure standing in front of her. Her eyes hungrily feasted on the naked torso, darkened with the mat of hair that swirled over flexed muscles, over the flat nipples, narrowing down the stomach, disappearing into the waistband of his swimming trunks. Unashamedly her eyes roved over his thighs, covered with dark curls and flexed taut, cords of muscle clearly outlined in the early morning light.

For the first time in her life she wanted to take a man's sensuality; she wanted to fondle him; she wanted to relieve the growing ache in her lower body; she wanted to fill her emptiness. Unbeknown to herself, her desire flashed in her eyes, and she licked her lips, the moisture forming a filmy sheen on them that tantalized Brendan, mesmerized him.

It was all he could do to keep his distance. Yet he must. He had to be content with her visual discovery of him. He couldn't push her too quickly. Later they could touch and discover the sweetness of each other. Later he could taste her mouth, nibble at her lips ... Later he could do all that he desired to do with her beautiful body. God! Could he wait until then?

He held his hand out. "Shall we go?" He had to get her out of this room before he lost control completely.

She nodded, dropping her hand into his. Together they walked out of the apartment and across the landscaped terrace to the swimming pool.

"I like those glasses," he commented lazily, seeking conversation. "I can see your eyes." He grinned. "There's nothing I hated more than talking to you without seeing your eyes."

Francyne chuckled, his casual tone and the warmth of the sun relaxing her, melting her inhibitions and doubts away. "I've annoyed you on several occasions then, haven't I?"

He nodded. "There was a time or two, but now"—He smiled mischievously into her eyes—"I would just take them off."

"I love the sun," Francyne declared, dropping the towels on the first lounger, dropping herself on the second. "I think I'll just sunbathe while you swim."

Brendan stared at her. "You don't think you're going to sit around the pool in that washcloth all day, do you?"

Francyne closed both eyes, shutting out the massive shadow of manhood that loomed up in front of her. "I might!"

"You might not!" he barked, taking a step in her direction.

She opened her eyes and grinned at him. "And what do you propose to do about it?"

"Dear one," he said in low tones, "don't play with fire unless you want to get burned."

"Maybe I've been trained in fire prevention," she retorted daringly, thrilled by her prowess as a woman, enchanted with the mild flirtation, anticipating the consummation of the courtship.

"Maybe you have," he said, his voice dangerously soft, his hands resting on his hips. "We'll see." The promise gleamed in his eyes, in the arrogance of his stance. "Right now we're going to swim. We'll fight the fire later." Hands on both hips, he stood. "Take the robe off, please." His voice commanded obedience.

Slowly she stood up; slowly she untied the white string that gathered the terry cloth around her waist, letting the white material billow from her shoulders. Removing her sunglasses, she meticulously folded the eyepieces and nestled them in the safety of one of the towels. Looking over her shoulder, she glanced furtively at Brendan.

"I'm still waiting," he said quietly from behind her. He moved forward, putting his hands on her shoulders, nesting his chin in the crook between her neck and shoulders. "I want to see you, sweetheart. I'm as curious about you as you were about me. There's nothing wrong with it; it's a natural reaction."

Francyne raised her shoulders in a half-shrug. "I know," she murmured, wondering why all of a sudden she should begin to act like an adolescent who had never had a boyfriend before.

It wasn't as if she'd never gone swimming in the presence of men before. She felt that the robe was the only thing that stood between her and him. When it came off, she would be virtually naked, not physically, but psychologically—and morally. She would become a part of him, a part of him that he would refuse to recognize. She would become a part of him that he might not be able to recognize.

Their morals were different; their outlooks on life were totally different. She wanted a husband, a family, a home. If not that, she did want the commitment of love. But Brendan had made no secret of his feelings about commitments. He wanted her, but he didn't want all of her. He wanted no commitments; he wanted no entanglements, no strings.

Brendan was standing patiently behind her, his hands still on her shoulders, his face still tucked in the warmth of her shoulder and neck. He couldn't understand her hesitancy, but he would play along. Time wasn't necessarily of the essence.

Her decision made, she swept out of his grasp, leaned down and caught the hem of the poncho with both hands, pulled it over her head, and threw it onto the lounge chair. She stood proudly in the mid-morning sun, her head held erect, her eyes a defiant blue-green that reflected the color of the leaves that surrounded the gardenias on her swimsuit.

As carefully as she had examined his body, Brendan studied hers. He studied it in detail, from the soft brown hair that billowed around her face, whispering over her shoulders, to the bare feet that were firmly planted on the tile by the edge of the swimming pool. His eyes raked up and down over the soft mounds of her breasts to the small waist, the flat tummy, the rounded hips, the suntanned thighs that gleamed like burnished copper.

Francyne couldn't tell much about what he was thinking because he had lowered that invisible barrier over his eyes, but when he spoke she could hear the gruff undertones of passion in his voice.

"I . . . " He paused, and his brown eyes lingered on the black suit, on the brightly splashed band of flowers that ran diagonally across her breasts and belly. "I've never seen a one-piece suit that was so—" Again he paused, and he shook his head. God, he thought disgustedly, this is a first for me. How can such a creature get to me like this? He'd never been tongue-tied before.

"So what?" Francyne prompted softly, inebriated with her ability to arouse him, to be provocative.

". . . so alluring," he finished, his voice dying to a whisper. "Maybe it . . ." The shutter over his eyes raised; he looked directly into hers, and for perhaps one of the few times in his life he didn't have to resort to exaggeration and insincerity. He could truthfully bare his soul to the woman whom he intended to claim so completely.

"Maybe it's what?" Francyne asked, recognizing the

99

passionate fire in his eyes, warming herself in the blaze, coming closer physically and spiritually.

"Maybe it's the woman wearing it," he said, as if in a hypnotic trance, his eyes still burning with intensity.

"Just maybe?" she whispered, cocking a finely shaped brow.

"No." He shook his head. "No, it's not just maybe. It's her all right."

Somehow they were together, and his arms were around her. He held her close to him, drinking of her strength, her goodness, her love. It wasn't a passionate embrace. It could have been, but it wasn't. It was a warm, comforting embrace, one that spoke of many more to come.

Without knowing Francyne, he knew her. With that knowledge came the assurance that she wouldn't give herself to him unless she loved him. Her love was defined by words like *husband, family, home, commitment, forever.* . . . Her kind of love was defined with all those words that he had excluded from his vocabulary.

Standing there, drinking in her presence, the light fragrance of her perfume, the clean freshness of her hair, the creamy smoothness of her skin, he realized that he cared. The thought staggered him; he was almost physically sickened by the discovery. Perhaps he did have a conscience after all.

He cared enough about her that he hesitated to impose his will on her; he hesitated to use his expertise as a lover to break down her rigid barriers of self-defense. If he went to bed with her, he would destroy them. When he eventually left her . . . and wasn't that inevitable? Had he ever found a woman who could keep his interest for more than a few months at the most? So . . . when he eventually left her, what would happen to her?

100

Uncomfortable with these thoughts and sensations, he suddenly pushed her away, grabbed her hand, and ran toward the water. He forced these unwelcome thoughts from his mind, thinking only of the present, of today, this minute. He forced himself to smile and avoided her eyes, which mirrored her perplexity and her hurt.

"Last one in is a rotten egg." And he dived in.

Puzzled by this abrupt change in his mood, Francyne followed slowly, gingerly stepping into the shallow water. Soon, however, she was splashing and playing with him in the water, her misgivings pushed aside for the time being. Although he tried to persuade her into the deeper water, she refused.

"I know when I'm in over my head," she retorted when she stood in water that came up to her bustline.

Eventually they got tired and wanted something cool to drink. Lying in separate reclining loungers, their eyes closed, each tried to persuade the other that it was his or her duty to go get something to drink, but they both were equally stubborn in their refusals. So neither of them moved until Francyne spoke again.

"I'm going to the apartment to fix myself a glass of iced tea." She shoved herself up lethargically, swinging her legs over the side of the chair. "If you want something, you'll have to come fix it, or go buy it." Holding her towel and robe in one hand, she picked up her thongs in the other.

"What else do you have to drink?" Brendan asked lazily, looking at her through half-closed eyes, his hands folded in back of his head.

"Coffee, lemonade . . ."

"Not exactly what I had in mind," he said, "but I guess it'll have to do. I don't plan to go buy anything right now." His lids fluttered down, his thick, curly lashes resting on the bronzed cheeks. "So I'll drink iced tea with you." With a litheness that betrayed the indolence in his voice, he pushed himself to his feet, slipping into his sandals. "Ready?"

She nodded, and they slowly trekked upstairs, not bothering to change clothes immediately. They walked into the kitchen, and Francyne, after dropping the towels and her robe on the table, began to fix a large pitcher of tea.

"Where's the kettle?" Brendan asked, looking in the cabinets around the stove.

"I use instant tea," Francyne informed him, opening a door and pulling out a large jar of brownish powder.

"Ugh!" Brendan grimaced. "I'm not overly fond of tea, and I certainly don't think I want instant tea."

"Fine with me," Francyne replied unconcernedly. "The tea bags are over there." She pointed to the canister. "And the tea leaves are in that cabinet. Use whichever you prefer." Over the running water, she said, "If you want brewed tea, you make it. I want instant, and that's what I'm making."

"Oh, I don't care," he said impatiently, grabbing the wet towels and robe. "I'll drink whatever you fix." He didn't like the gloating smirk that Francyne flashed in his direction. "Do you want me to throw these in the dryer or over the curtain rod in the bathroom?"

"Put them in the dryer," she said, turning off the spigot and lifting the pitcher from the sink. "It's in the bathroom."

He nodded, walking out of the room. "I'm going to change."

When the tea was ready, Francyne cut a lemon and put the slices in a small bowl, which she placed on a tray beside the pitcher and two glasses of ice. She carried the tray into the living room, setting it on the cocktail table before she ducked into her bedroom to shuck her wet swimsuit. She slipped quickly into a pair of bikini panties and a short romper suit of white terry cloth that was gathered above her breasts with no more than an elastic band.

A little daring, isn't it, Francyne? She stepped back and surveyed the effect. She looked at the bare shoulders; she looked at the top that barely covered her breasts; she looked at the length of leg that was revealed by the skimpy outfit.

Maybe not, she lied to herself, brushing her wet hair, letting it hang loosely so it would dry. I've worn it before and never thought it was so revealing. You've never been alone in your apartment with a man who stirs you up like Brendan does either, she argued. But, she retorted, I can take care of myself. I've done it in the past, haven't I? In the past, yes! What about now—today? I can handle it. She padded barefoot across the floor into the living room, all arguments resolved . . . at least, pushed aside for the time being. She would wear the romper suit.

Standing by the window, wearing his jeans with his shirt unbuttoned and hanging loosely, Brendan held a half-empty glass of iced tea in his hand. When he heard the door faintly open and close, he turned and watched as she walked into the room. His mouth tightened, and the muscles flexed as he clenched his teeth. Quite a change from the prude of a minute ago! It seemed like an open invitation. But he couldn't believe that was her style.

She didn't have her glasses on, but she could tell by his stance and by the narrowed eyes that, once again, he wasn't pleased with her choice. She wished she could dart into the bedroom and change into her jeans and shirt, but that would call even more attention to her scanty outfit.

She forced herself to smile. Try to act naturally, she told herself, walking over to the cocktail table. "How do you like the tea?" He nodded curtly. "I thought you would," she quipped, pouring herself a glass and squeezing lemon into it.

As she sat down he turned his back to her and stared out the window. He put one hand on his hip, drawing his shirt back from his torso. All his resolve was deserting him; he wanted her. And her flaunting herself in front of him didn't help. Dear Lord, he wondered, does she have any idea what she's doing to me?

"I think you'd better go put something on, and let's get out of here." The words were as clipped as his nod had been.

"You don't like it?"

Dear God, he'd never understand women. "It's not a matter of my liking it. It's a matter of how much the two of us can bear." He turned around suddenly. "What is this? An endurance contest? How much can Brendan stand before he loses control?"

Francyne didn't pretend to misunderstand him.

"Go get dressed, and we'll go to lunch."

She nodded.

"If you don't"—his voice changed, taking on a caressing tone—"I won't be responsible for what the two of us will do." The brown eyes were appealing in their supplication. "Do you understand what I'm saying?"

She nodded, slowly putting her glass down on the table, moving in the direction of her room. Then with a boldness that astonished her, she said, "I . . . I'm responsible for what I do, not you!" Defiance held her head erect and her back straight as she walked out of the room.

In her bedroom she jerked open the closet, grabbed the first thing she saw, and yanked it off the hanger, tears blinding her. She knew he was right; they couldn't stay here any longer without making love, but she didn't want to leave. She wanted him. *She wanted him!*

She threw the dress on the chest at the end of the bed and walked to the dresser to get herself a bra. Then she heard the gentle swish of the door as it brushed against the carpet. Looking into the mirror she saw Brendan, leaning on the closed door. Her breath caught in her throat, and she stood still, her hands clenched at her sides.

Neither of them moved; they just stared at each other. For a moment time stood still. Yet during this silence his eyes asked the question. During this silence her eyes answered it. There was no doubt or hesitancy.

He pushed his nagging conscience aside. She wants me and she knows what she's doing, he told himself. Why not? Both of us will enjoy it.

With a quick motion, he pushed away from the door and shrugged out of his shirt, dropping it at his feet. Then he unfastened his jeans, unzipping them, never taking his eyes off her reflection in the mirror. Mesmerized, she watched him kick out of them, letting them fall over the shirt. He stood with his legs straddled, his hands resting on his hips.

Francyne's eyes, large and fathomless, gazed at the hair-darkened chest, the strong arms, the narrow waist and hips, the powerful legs. Catching her eyes in the mirror, Brendan smiled, and her heart skipped a beat—she felt that it had actually turned over in her chest.

His hands, palms sliding down his torso, slid beneath the elastic of his shorts, and he pushed them over his hips and down his thighs, kicking out of them. Now he stood, and she unashamedly viewed his nakedness. She couldn't have torn her eyes away even if she had wanted to. She watched him move across the carpet until he was standing behind her.

"I'm not going to fight it," he confessed, his lips burning kisses into her bare shoulders. "I want you. God help me, Francyne, but I want you."

Did he turn her around? Did she turn to him herself? She didn't know, she didn't care, as long as she was in his arms. Her face was cradled against his chest, her cheek nuzzling the flexed muscles, soft murmurs escaping her parted lips. Then he guided her to the bed, setting her down gently on the coverlet, sliding in beside her, his hands and his mouth telling her of his tormenting needs and desires.

He pushed her hair out of her face, tucking it back behind her ears; his lips planted small kisses from her ears down the side of her neck and across her collar bone to the sensitive skin just above the elastic band on her romper suit. He nipped the skin, wanting to taste her, to discover the honeyed essence of her body.

His hot, moist lips drew away, and she felt as if a path had been burned into her skin. Then those same burning lips captured hers in a soul-searching kiss, designed to discover her most secret self. His lips opened hers, his tongue sought each cavern of delight, dislodging her own, pillaging and plundering until she groaned her deep-seated needs.

Her hands at a frenzied pitch tangled in the thick curls, and she pressed his face closer to hers, not tasting enough, wanting more, hungry for the feel and the taste of his body. The kisses were prolonged and became more intoxicating and at the same time kindled a fire in her pelvis that slowly flamed higher and higher. She was excruciatingly aware of her emptiness, and his probing tongue only helped to make her awareness more acute.

As their bodies writhed on the bed, her top slid lower and lower until her breasts were exposed, and his hands were reverently fondling them. His thumb circled the passion-crested tip of one, and his mouth encircled the other. His tongue curled around the tip, stroking, drawing back, waiting for her thrust, stroking again, then slowly moving around the tip. Then he suckled, tenderly, sweetly, and she melted in his arms.

All inhibitions were burned away. Nothing remained but clothing to separate them, and it was easily discarded. A yank, a wiggle, a toss, and both of them were lying together, naked, feeling, searching, finding, wanting. . . .

She wanted him. She loved him. There would be no holding back. There would be no denial. Perhaps later there would be recriminations . . . perhaps . . . but not now.

His body arched above hers, and his hands delighting her, tantalizing her, adoringly prepared her for their total union. In the midst of the whispered endearments, the ragged breathing, the frenzied movements they heard the loud clanging of the doorbell. Both lay still, startled out of their blissful abandon. They listened, hoping they wouldn't hear the bell again. But their wish didn't come true.

"Who could that be?" Brendan grated harshly.

Francyne rolled her head back and forth on the pillow. "I don't know." The bell chimed again. "I'm not expecting anyone." She paused. "Just Mom."

Again the bell rang, this time longer, more insistently.

"Just Mom!" Francyne's words reverberated in the

bedroom. "I'll bet that's Mom!" she screeched, sliding out from underneath Brendan's upraised weight.

"Francyne!" The call filtered softly through the door.

"My God! It is Mom! What will she think?"

Muttering a few choice expletives, Brendan rolled off the bed, dragged across the room, and gathered up his clothes, pulling them on. In the meantime the chiming of the doorbell wouldn't stop.

"For God's sake," Brendan snapped, "tell her that you're coming, Francyne. That damned bell is driving me crazy."

Francyne nodded, running to the door and opening it. "Just a minute, Mom," she called. "I'm coming." Without picking up her panties, she pulled the romper suit over her thighs and above her breasts, adjusting the elastic. She started to leave the room.

"Brush your hair," Brendan commanded dryly. "It's a tangled mess."

"Thanks," she muttered ungratefully, giving her hair two or three swipes with the brush.

"And get hold of yourself," he snapped. "After all, this is your apartment and your life. Surely your mother doesn't still dictate your morals to you. You're nearly twenty-eight, aren't you?"

His anger restored Francyne's composure more quickly than anything else could have done. "No," she spat back at him, "my mother doesn't dictate my morals, but I certainly don't intend to have her and Keeley walk in here to find you and me in the bed in the middle of . . . in the middle of—"

"Thanks to them," he snorted in disgust, "in the middle of nothing." He walked out of the bedroom.

"Where are you going?" Francyne cried in panic.

"To get some coffee," he replied shortly. "It's the

108

strongest drink in the house." He slammed the door after him.

Relieved that he was staying, but not looking forward to greeting her mother, Francyne walked into the living room and opened the door.

"What took you so long?" Sylvia demanded. She was clutching a shopping bag in her hands, and her eyes raked over her daughter, taking in the flushed cheeks, the disheveled hair, the eyes that wouldn't quite meet hers.

"Golly, Franny," Keeley complained, following her grandmother through the door, "you didn't have to take so long before you answered the door."

"I decided to bring Keeley home earlier," Sylvia explained, her eyes sweeping over the apartment, "because your Dad and I want to drive down to—" She paused, her voice lapsing into silence as she spied the two glasses with their melting cubes of ice, the condensation running down the sides. Then she looked back at Francyne, taking in her state of undress. She never completed the sentence.

"You . . . you had company?"

"Have company," Francyne corrected heavily, walking to the cocktail table, pouring herself a glass of tea. She looked at her mother. "Care for a glass?"

Sylvia slowly shook her head, crumpling the paper bag in her hands. "Brendan?"

Francyne could imagine her thoughts as they flickered in Sylvia's mind, flaring like large neon signs in her eyes. She saw her mother's blue eyes flit nervously to the bedroom door.

"He's in the kitchen," Francyne stated flatly.

Sylvia sighed, and Keeley squealed with delight, darting into the kitchen to leave Francyne alone with her mother.

Sylvia held up the white bag. "I brought these jeans that you wanted to have altered." She briskly walked toward Francyne's bedroom. "I want you to try them on." She pushed open the door and moved over to the dresser, taking the jeans out of the bag. "I think they'll be okay." Her eyes took in the mussed covers on the bed; then she saw the discarded panties lying on the far side of the bed. She looked at Francyne, hurt and disappointment darkening her blue eyes. Silently she accused her daughter.

Francyne quietly defended herself. "I . . . I love him, Mom."

"Does love make it all right?" Sylvia asked in a small, tight voice.

"I wouldn't go to bed with a man for less than love," Francyne replied, her voice low but steady.

"You hardly know him," Sylvia objected, in that soft, sweet voice that usually preceded one of her outbursts. "Two days!"

"I still love him," Francyne said stubbornly, her eyes directly on her mother's face. She was a grown woman and had her own life, but somehow, confronting her mother like this made her feel like a teenager. Only when Sylvia lowered her eyes did Francyne walk to the dresser to pick up her jeans.

"I . . . I don't pretend to understand today's permissive society," Sylvia began, "much less condone it, but" —Francyne could hear the censure in her mother's tones—"it seems that this is the way it's done nowadays. I . . . I . . ." She turned to Francyne, her voice wavering. "I don't mean to interfere in your life—you know I never have. I just don't want you to be hurt." Tears caused the blue eyes to shimmer. "Please," she begged with all her maternal powers of persuasion, "be careful."

110

"I will, Mom," Francyne replied, her hands balling into fists, closing over the fabric of her jeans.

"Do you plan to marry him?"

Do I plan to marry him? Francyne thought. How ironic! The question is, Does he plan to marry me?

"Francyne," Sylvia pleaded, her voice suggesting hysteria, "do you plan to marry him?"

Francyne couldn't answer.

"Does . . . does he love you?" Sylvia persisted, as only a doting mother can.

Francyne's head was bowed over her dresser, and she still didn't answer. "I don't know," she said softly, after a long pause.

"Oh, Francyne." Sylvia almost wept, walking over to her daughter, putting her arms around her. "Do you know what you're doing?"

Francyne nodded. "I know what I'm doing, but I'm not sure what the outcome will be."

Sylvia nodded her head slowly, knowing that although she wanted to impose her will on Francyne, wanted to impart her maternal wisdom to her, she couldn't. Francyne was a mature woman, capable of making her own decisions. Now, as her mother, Sylvia knew that she must be silent. She must let Francyne lead her own life and make and live with her own decisions.

Gathering her scattered wits, she said, "I—your dad and I—we like Brendan." She wiped her eyes with her fingertips. "He . . . he seems to be a nice young man."

Almost in tears herself, Francyne only nodded.

Sylvia looked at her watch and cleared her throat. "Dad's waiting at the house, so I guess I'd better hurry. We want to get on the road as soon as possible." She looked at the jeans. "When you get a chance, try them on, and if they don't fit, I'll work on them some more."

111

Francyne turned to face Sylvia. "Okay," she mumbled.

Sylvia nodded and walked to the door, twisting the knob but not pulling the door open. "Do you—" She hesitated, then asked, "Do you want me to take Keeley with us?"

Ironically Francyne laughed at the same time that two tears rolled down her cheeks. She shook her head and wiped her eyes. "No, I don't want you to take Keeley with you." She grinned. "Nothing happened, Mom. Nothing."

"I'm glad," Sylvia whispered, looking directly into those huge, warm eyes. "Just remember to be careful, Francyne," she said, lowering her voice to a husky whisper. "I don't want you hurt."

She walked out of the bedroom, followed by Francyne, and didn't stop until she had opened the living room door. Unexpectedly she smiled. "Perhaps if I were young like you and had a good-looking guy like Brendan, I might, I just might"—she emphasized the last three words and paused—"be tempted also." Then she closed the door.

Francyne was left standing in the middle of the room, smiling to herself, glad to have an understanding mother. Finally she moved over to the window and stood staring at the people who were congregating around the pool. Too much had happened today, and she couldn't think anymore, so she just watched. She didn't even move until she heard the kitchen door glide over the carpet.

Keeley danced into the room. "Glad I came back early, Franny?"

Francyne looked beyond Keeley to the man who stood leaning against the doorjamb. She nodded, never taking her eyes off him. "Yes, I'm glad that you came

112

back early." Her answer was as much for Brendan as it was for the child.

"How about you, Brendan?" Keeley taunted, dancing around him also. "Are you glad?"

"Nothing could have made me happier." His tone was gentle, but his brown eyes met Francyne's, letting her read his irritation and frustration.

"Now we can have some fun," Keeley said impishly, her eyes glowing with delight.

Francyne began to grin when Brendan's scowl deepened, and then she chuckled softly.

"Oh, shut up," he said crossly to Francyne as he pushed away from the doorjamb. "It's not that funny!"

CHAPTER FIVE

As soon as she opened the door to her apartment Francyne slipped out of her shoes, picked them up, and walked through the bedroom into her walk-in closet, which was part of her large bathroom–dressing room. She tucked her shoes into the shoe rack and unfastened her skirt, stepping out of it. After she hung it up, she unclasped the gold chain from around her neck and put it on the dresser, walking out of the room. On her way to the kitchen she began to unbutton her blouse.

She was glad that the day was over. She was beat! As usual Monday was a hectic day from beginning to end, and Roberta's being gone hadn't helped matters. Because she was short one tour guide, Francyne had recruited herself for a tour that had taken most of the afternoon and the early evening. Now she was looking forward to a nice relaxing bath and a late dinner with Brendan. Just the thought of him brought a smile to her lips and relieved some of the weariness of the day.

She pulled on the cabinet door and reached for a glass; then she moved to the refrigerator to fill it with ice and tea. She was squeezing lemon into it when the phone rang. Holding the receiver with one hand, she shrugged out of her blouse with the other.

"Hello."

"Hello, sweetheart. Finally make it in?"

Collapsing on the nearest barstool, she wilted happily, loving the sonorous voice that flowed through the line. It was hard for her to believe that she'd just left him a few hours ago, that they'd lunched together as usual on the river.

"Umhumm," she sighed, thinking of their evening together. It wouldn't matter what they did. She would just enjoy being with him. "Just got in."

He chuckled. "I know it. I've been calling about every fifteen or twenty minutes. These guys think I'm nuts."

Francyne smiled, happiness radiating through her body, slowing on her face, in her eyes, in her lips. "I'm glad you called."

"I miss you," he softly sighed, his confession sensuously exciting to the woman on the other end of the line.

"I miss you too," she replied. "I can hardly wait to see you."

"That's what I called about," he said slowly. She heard a phone ring in the background. He sighed and muttered a soft expletive. "Just a minute, hon. Let me get the other phone. I'm expecting an important call."

Francyne sipped her tea, listening to the faraway noises of the office in the background, catching a few words that Brendan spoke.

Suddenly she heard "You still there?"

"Umhumm," she said, swallowing a mouthful of tea.

"I'm sorry, sweetheart, but I've got to work late

115

tonight. These negotiations are top priority, and I can't stop now."

"Oh, Brendan," she said softly; her eyes shimmered with tears of disappointment.

"Oh, yes," he replied with a tender chuckle. "Now you know how I felt when you called that time to tell me that you were working late and couldn't meet me for dinner. Remember?"

"I remember," Francyne admitted, "but it doesn't make it any easier."

"I know, honey, and I wouldn't break our date if it weren't so important."

"I know," she quickly inserted. "I was just looking forward to a happy ending to an otherwise miserable afternoon." Suddenly an idea struck her. "How about your coming over for dinner or a snack or whatever after you get through tonight?"

"I'll be over for the *or whatever*," Brendan said without hesitation. "That sounds better than any offer I've had from you so far."

"Oh, Brendan," Francyne gurgled indignantly, stifling her laughter, "you always twist around everything I say."

He laughed, the lazy tones, rich and mellow, filling Francyne with an exhilaration she'd never felt before. "I don't know how much longer I'm going to be, and it's already pretty late."

"I don't mind," Francyne assured him. "I usually sit up quite late."

"What if I'm so tired when I get there that I want to go to bed?" he asked, grinning at the expression he could imagine on her face.

"I do have a guest room," she informed him in a small, demure voice.

116

He chuckled, and in the background someone called out his name. "Come on, Brendan. We need you."

He sighed. "I've got to go, sweetheart. They've got their coffee and had a smoke, so we're ready to hit the drawing board again. Tell you what. If we're through by eleven, I'll drop by. Otherwise I'll call you in the morning."

"In the morning," she grumbled, not wanting to wait that long.

He lowered his voice. "If I'm going to sleep alone, I'd just as soon do it in my own bed." He heard her breathy laugh. "I'll call in the morning for sure, and we'll have lunch together for sure. Same place, same time!"

"Okay," she murmured.

"Brendan, come on!" Francyne could hear a man's voice bellowing in the background.

"Keep tomorrow evening free, okay?"

She whispered, "Okay," and gently replaced the receiver after he'd hung up, the happy anticipation of her evening gone.

While she was puttering around in the kitchen she decided to salvage the remnants of a large picnic ham. She diced it into small pieces and dropped it into a pot full of boiling lima beans. While the beans and ham were cooking she mixed a pone of cornbread, sliding it into the oven. She might drink instant tea, but she didn't like instant food. And she was very much like her mother—a country girl at heart. She enjoyed the simple pleasures of country cooking.

No need to waste time, she thought, slightly dispirited. Might as well bring my log up to date. Walking into the bedroom, she pulled her slip off and stepped into a comfortable pair of old jeans and dropped an almost worn-out cotton shirt over her head. Moving to her desk, she opened the top of her attaché case and sorted through the papers, getting out her logbook before returning to the kitchen.

She worked steadily into the night, taking time out only to eat. Finally, however, when her back had begun to ache and her eyes were burning, she knew it was time to quit. She looked over her shoulder at the clock. Midnight!

She stood up and stretched, collected the dirty dishes, rinsed them off, and put them in the dishwasher. Brendan must still be in the meeting. She sighed her disappointment. Well, she thought, drying her hands and hanging the dishrag on the rack, she was at least caught up with her work. She neatly stacked her papers and took them into the bedroom, replacing them in the attaché case.

Because it was so late—not because she was sleepy— she decided to take a bath and go to bed. Moving through the apartment, she cut off the lights, checked to see that the stove was turned off, and double-checked the locks on the door and windows. Assured that all was well, she padded into the bedroom, peering at the clock one more time. Twelve thirty!

She wished he'd call. She wished he'd come on over.

She took off her shirt, slipped out of her jeans, and left both garments on her quilt rack. She'd hang them up in the morning. Right now she would take her bath and go to bed. In the bathroom she filled the tub with warm water, added her favorite bath oil—one that Sophie had given to her—and stepped in to soak for a long time.

Later she dried on the soft, nubby towel, rubbing herself until her skin was pink and tingling. Reaching behind the door, she pulled her nightgown from the peg, letting the soft fabric float over her head and cover

118

her body. Maybe she'd read for a while. That usually lulled her to sleep.

She desperately tried to get interested in her book, but she couldn't. Her mind wasn't on a murder mystery; it was on Brendan O'Shea. She laid her head against the stacked pillows, letting her mind wander in the verdant pastures of daydreams with him. As she allowed her imagination to run wild, the book slipped unheeded from her hands and slid to the floor, and when the doorbell clanged loudly, she jumped.

She looked at the clock. One thirty! Her heart began to beat louder and louder, faster and faster. It could only be Brendan! It had to be him! He had come after all. She jumped off the bed and scampered into the living room before she realized that she was in her nightgown. The bell rang again. She darted to the closet, opened the door, and grabbed her red robe off the hanger. As she raced to let him in she hopped first on one foot, then on the other as she pulled on her robe. At the door she released one lock and opened it a crack, zipping the front of her robe at the same time.

"Who's there?" she asked, happiness causing her voice to tremble.

"The big, bad wolf come to ravish Little Red Riding Hood." The husky tones that so easily jarred Francyne's sense of stability made her poignantly aware of her growing attraction for Brendan O'Shea.

"I didn't expect you this late," she babbled, clumsily working the other lock, yanking the door open.

He smiled patiently, peering in through the crack. "I'll leave if you want me to."

"Of course not," Francyne said in a shocked whisper. "I didn't mean that. I wanted you to come."

"Good," he returned, "I wanted to see you too. That's why I decided to come over instead of calling."

119

The door glided open, and he walked in. Francyne stared at him as if she'd never seen him before. She luxuriated in his presence, and even though he looked tired, he was more devastating than she had remembered. His white shirt was unbuttoned at the neck, revealing that small mat of dark hair and the chain. His tie, still knotted, hung loosely around his collar. His suit jacket was carelessly slung over his left shoulder, precariously hitched between his thumb and folded fingers.

He threw the jacket over the pier-glass-and-table set in the foyer and reached for her at the same time. He caught her in his arms, thrusting his face into the creamy curve of her shoulder, smelling the clean fragrance of her shampoo and bath oil, inhaling deeply of the odor that lightly tantalized his senses, making him more than aware of his desires.

"I couldn't let the night go by without seeing you," he murmured.

"I'm glad," Francyne replied, her hands already tangled in the rich thickness of his hair. "I wanted to see you too."

"You smell good," he said, and she could hear the weariness in his voice. "What kind of perfume do you have on?"

She told him. "It's some that Sophie gave me. Like it?"

She felt his head as it moved against her shoulder; she felt his hands as they feathered down her spine, molding the curve of her buttocks with outstretched fingers. "Umhumm," he chanted softly. "It tells me to take you to bed with me."

Francyne chuckled. "It may tell you that, but I haven't."

"That's what I thought you'd say," he returned, pulling himself away. "Got anything to eat or drink?" He followed Francyne's eyes to the bar. He shook his head. "Not that. I need nourishment at the moment. I'm bone-weary."

"I have some tea," she said tentatively, knowing his aversion to instant tea. She grinned when she saw the familiar grimace. "I could brew you some coffee though."

"Now, that, my girl, is a brilliant suggestion. I'd like that very much." Solemnly he lifted one eyebrow and looked at her questioningly. "I take it that this isn't instant coffee?"

Francyne chortled and moved in the direction of her bedroom to get her glasses. "That's what the word *brew* implies," she retorted. She spun the rack that held her many pairs of glasses, finding the frames that she wanted. She was putting them on when she heard Brendan speak from the door.

"You're an optician on the side?"

"Not really," she qualified. "I just like glasses, and I like to be coordinated." She adjusted the frames on her nose. "Since I've only myself to please, and to support, I indulge my whims."

He stood by the dresser and twirled the rack. "Someone really gave you a complex about these, didn't he?"

She shrugged and gave him a half-smile. "Perhaps." She remembered a few painful memories from childhood, but nothing serious.

Not understanding his feelings, he suddenly felt the pain of a child who has been ridiculed or teased; he felt Francyne's pain. He didn't like this moment of empathy with her at all. It made him feel too vulnerable. It made them a part of one another. He drew her toward him, pressing her face against his chest, and she could feel the wiry hairs through the thin fabric of his shirt.

121

"Tell me about it." His voice was tender with concern and understanding.

She nodded. "As a teenager I was in competition with a lovely older sister. Not her fault, you understand, but my dates would invariably fall in love with her and out of love with me." She laughed, the husky sounds exciting him. "So I equated that with my glasses." When he started to say something, she leaned back and gazed into his face, pressing her finger to his mouth. "I outgrew that, but when I finally got into high school—" She paused, remembering, and her body began to shake with laughter.

Brendan didn't wait to look at her face or her eyes. He caught her to him and pressed her face against his chest again. He thought she was crying from hurt and humiliation. His embrace tightened, and he murmured incoherent endearments in her ear. Not wanting to spoil the tenderness of the moment, Francyne suppressed her laughter and basked in the joy of his caring.

"What happened?" he asked.

"I had a precious teacher by the name of Miss Higgins." Her voice nearly cracked with suppressed laughter. "Miss Higgins was a wizard when it came to math, but she wore the most awful glasses that I'd ever seen. The kids laughed and made fun of her most of the time. And I promised myself that I would never wear old-fashioned or frumpy glasses unless I had to. And so far I haven't had to." She pulled back and looked into her face. "Fooled you, didn't I? You thought I had some terrible complex about glasses, and you, Dr. O'Shea, were going to cure me."

He should have been angry, he thought. What had been a tender moment for him—a moment that had even caused him to see another side of himself—was no more than a chance for flippancy for her. Yet he couldn't be angry. She meant that much to him. He knit his brows, however, and scowled at her. As she turned, dancing out of his arms, he slapped her on the buttocks.

"And that, Francyne LaRue," he said when she turned to glare at him, cupping her bottom with both hands, "should teach you to be impertinent with me. Now get to the galley, wench, and fix me some coffee and food."

It wasn't long before Francyne had the coffee maker filled with water and grounds, and the aroma of freshly perked coffee was filtering through the kitchen. Brendan sat at the breakfast table, watching Francyne's leisurely efficiency. He could tell that she was comfortable in the kitchen; she enjoyed preparing a meal for him.

He sniffed appreciatively. "That coffee smells delicious. I haven't eaten since lunch, and I'm famished."

"I have some lima beans and ham with cornbread," Francyne announced, peering into the open refrigerator. "Or some cold cuts for sandwiches, or I can fix some bacon and eggs and toast."

"If you don't mind, I'll take the bacon and some scrambled eggs."

Francyne nodded, took the plastic egg keeper out of the refrigerator, and set it on the stove. "Scrambled eggs and bacon coming up."

"Lima beans and ham," Brendan repeated pensively. "Is that another LaRue specialty?"

Francyne laughed with him, shaking her head. "No, just some good old country cooking that we happen to enjoy. You might say it's a Sylvia favorite. But," she added, pulling a large pie plate from the refrigerator, "I do have another LaRue speciality. How about some fresh apple pie, baked from scratch?"

"Now that sounds like my kind of eating," he declared.

Not being hungry herself, Francyne cooked only for Brendan, and while he ate she drank a glass of tea. Sporadically, between bites, he asked her about her day, and she regaled him with a full account. After the eggs and bacon, a slice of pie, and a cup of coffee Brendan pushed his plate aside.

"Thanks," he said, "I really needed this tender loving care." He pushed his chair back, stood, and walked to the counter, refilling his cup for a second time.

"Aren't you afraid of staying awake all night?" Francyne asked.

"I will be," he announced flatly. He twisted his wrist, looking at his watch.

"You've got to go back?" Francyne asked, appalled by the idea.

He lifted the cup to his lips and drank deeply before he spoke again. Even then he spoke hesitantly. "I've got to leave for Dallas tonight."

"Dallas," Francyne murmured unbelievingly. "You're leaving for Dallas tonight?"

He nodded. "I've got to be in Houston, El Paso, Beaumont, Baton Rouge, and back to Beaumont before next weekend."

Her face reflected her hurt and disappointment. In a small, tight voice she whispered, "That means you won't be here for my birthday!"

He set the cup down on the counter, returned to the table, and sat down across from her. He looked at the golden-brown hair that fell against her ashen cheeks. He looked at those eyes which could be blue or brown or green or gold, but were always beautiful to him. He reached across the table and traced the outline of her eyebrows, causing her to lower the thick sooty curtain of her lashes.

"I love those thick eyelashes," he said softly, watching the faint color mounting in her cheeks. Then he added, "I wouldn't go if it weren't vitally important. I want to be here for your birthday."

His fingers never stopped tracing, and the simple caress drugged Francyne and left her nothing more than a mass of churning emotions. Out of habit she started to play with her glasses, which lay on the table in front of her glass. She reached up and rubbed her fingers across her eyes. She didn't want him to see her tears.

"Do you believe me?"

She nodded, chewing her bottom lip. "I believe you." Then she asked, "When are you leaving?"

"Tonight," he replied quietly.

"When will you be back?"

"In time for work on Monday morning."

She smiled tightly, pulling her face away from the sensuous assault of his hands. She began to gather up the dishes and to stack them. Without another word she stood up and carried them to the sink. But she couldn't go on. She simply stood there, her back to Brendan, on the verge of tears. Then she felt him right behind her.

"Francyne—"

She could hear the hesitancy in his voice, and she knew he was going to say something about them— about him and her. She didn't know what he would say, but she knew it would mark a change in their relationship.

"I didn't want to break our date tonight. It meant a lot to me. You mean a lot to me."

She could hear the concern in his voice. He cared

about her, and he was letting her know it. But how much deeper than that did it go?

"But being with you on your birthday means more to me than our date tonight. Your birthday is something special to me because you're special to me."

She smiled, and her heart increased its pace again, making her draw her breath in sharply. He had remembered.

"We'll celebrate when you get back," she promised, her voice husky and vibrant.

"I don't want to celebrate when I get back," he said, lowering his voice, sending seductive vibes through her body. "I want to celebrate your birthday with you, on your birthday." He let the words sink in. "I'd . . . I'd like you to join me in Beaumont next weekend."

She hadn't expected this, and she didn't answer because she couldn't. Shock had left her tongue-tied. Knowing what Brendan wanted out of their relationship was one thing, but for him to actually put it into words was more than she could handle. She had never realized before just how sheltered her life had been up to this point. At twenty-eight years of age, she suddenly realized, she didn't know how to cope with adult situations.

Finally she stammered, "I . . . I . . ."

"Don't tell me that you don't want to be with me," Brendan broke in impatiently. "It's something that both of us want, and we both know it." He knew that it was only a matter of time before she capitulated, and now he wanted her so badly that his body ached with longing.

She nodded her head, still not saying anything, not committing herself.

"I promise you a beautiful birthday, sweetheart."

"I . . . I don't know," she whispered, her heart telling her to say yes, her mind telling her to refuse.

"Give it a try."

When she didn't answer, he caught her shoulders roughly and whirled her around, winding his arms around her and drawing her closer to him. Hers lips instinctively lifted to meet his, and she quickly enveloped his body in her arms, loving the feel of him— strong, masculine, hard.

His mouth moved on hers, asking, questing, probing. Hers moved in answer, parting when his tongue swirled inside to make her groan with unspeakable delight. His lips were soft, and warm, and damp, surrounding her with the burning brand of his flesh as he pressed closer to her, denying her that fire when he pulled away. His tongue, his mouth, both needed the moist, pungent richness of hers and couldn't stay away for long.

He pulled her closer to him, grinding their flesh together, his hand sliding down her back to rest on her rounded buttocks. When he had acquainted her with the throbbing needs of his body, his lips lifted from hers and he rained tiny kisses over her face from her eyes to her nose to her cheeks back to her mouth. All the time his hands minutely explored the small of her back, the tight indentation of her buttocks.

He maneuvered so that he was leaning against the counter, and she was lying on top of him. His thigh slipped in between her legs, pressing warmly against her. His fevered hands opened her robe, the zipper gliding down without hindrance, and they explored, discovered, revealed, and caressed her swollen breasts. His fingers gently closed over a hardened nipple, and she softly moaned with pleasure.

She was breathing raggedly, moving against the heated hardness of his body. Sensuously she moved; sensuously she excited him. Her hands kneaded the flexed muscles in his back; her fingernails raked against the sinewy hardness.

Their passion ignited, the blaze consuming all within its path, and neither Brendan nor Francyne was willing to get out of its way. Each willingly lost himself in the inferno, delighting in the fiery emotions, the searing, white-hot light of desire.

Brendan's head lowered, and Francyne could hear him murmuring endearments as he fondled her breasts, pressing them together tenderly before he covered both of them with his mouth. Then his hot, moist lips closed over one nipple, stroking, brushing, arousing her to the point of no return. Her head was flung back, and she gasped for breath in tiny pants, her hands still circled around his waist.

She was languid with desire as his lips ravished and plundered. She moaned softly; then he lifted his lips, feathering kisses from her breasts up to her mouth. She moved against his hardness, reveling in her ability to arouse him, glorying in her womanhood when she heard him moan huskily.

He scooped her into his arms and moved toward the bed. He laid her down and knelt down beside her, the mattress sagging beneath his weight. She was on her back, looking into his face with passion-glazed eyes. He was on his side, propped on his arm. He drew her to him and kissed her again and again until she felt that she was burned to a crisp in the passionate fire that was consuming both of them.

"Meet me in Beaumont next week." He wasn't asking, nor was he pleading. His voice was soft and intimate, but this was unmistakably a command. He nuzzled his face in the creamy curve of her shoulder and neck. "I promise you won't regret it, my darling."

"I . . ." She drew a deep breath. "I need to think about it." The murmur was soft.

This wasn't quite the answer that he'd hoped for, but it was better than a flat no. There was room for persuasion. He glanced at the clock on the nightstand. Did he have time for persuasion? Hardly! He'd have to play his last hand. Win or lose, it was all he had left in this short time.

He pulled her robe together and zipped it up. "There," he teased, "we'll put temptation out of the way for the time being." He rolled off the bed and walked toward the living room. "Wait right there," he called over his shoulder. "I have something for you."

When he returned, he was carrying his jacket in one hand and a colored envelope in the other. He threw the jacket down on the end of the bed and handed her the envelope. She took it, looked at it, then raised her eyes to his inquiringly.

He spoke, his voice low but steady. "That's in case you decide to come."

She looked down at the plane ticket in her hand.

"If you decide to come, you can call me." He pointed to the bold black printing on the outside of the envelope. "That's my number and the hotel where I'll be staying."

"I . . . I don't know," she murmured.

He smiled. "Think about it." He picked up his jacket, fumbled through the pockets, and brought out a small jeweler's box. "In case you don't come," he said, "I want to give you your birthday present now."

She pushed herself up on the bed and stared as he flipped the box into her lap.

"I bought this for you."

With trembling fingers she picked up the box and opened the lid. She saw the gold chain, delicately fashioned with a lover's knot suspended in the center. She could hardly swallow the lump in her throat. She could hardly breathe for the constriction. She bit her lower lip.

"Oh, Brendan," she cried, trying to take the chain out of its bed of velvet. "It's beautiful."

She remembered their wandering in and out of the shops during noon, window-shopping for a necklace. She had liked this one in particular, but it had been too expensive for her to buy.

"This belongs to a special collection," the saleswoman had told her. She held the delicate chain over her outstretched fingers. "We have this one for a woman, and this one"—she picked up another necklace, a little heavier, a little bolder, and held it up—"is for a man. Today many engaged couples want necklaces as well as the traditional engagement ring," the woman added. "Some prefer it to the ring because they both can wear one."

Francyne lifted her eyes to his face, her love shining through for him to see. "You remembered," she said.

He nodded. "I remembered."

It was his nature to remember. He studied the woman he was interested in, to discover what made her tick, to know what she liked, to know what she didn't like, to understand her in order to manipulate her, to plan his next move. He had spent years perfecting the complicated art of seduction. Yet in all his life he had never once begun to understand the simplicity of falling in love, of pleasing a woman simply because he wanted to, not because he had some ulterior motive.

For the first time in his adult life, however, he felt the full impact of his deviousness and craftiness. He felt a twinge of remorse. But to give him credit, he hadn't been listening to the saleswoman when she explained the deeper meaning of the chains. He had been too busy scheming at the moment. Even he wouldn't have deliberately given Francyne this particular chain. Not even to seduce her would he have given her the false impression that the necklace spoke of something that might be. It was no more than a beautiful, expensive birthday gift for the woman whom he wanted as a lover. But Francyne didn't know this. . . .

"Put it around my neck," she commanded, scooting over on the bed, turning her back to him.

Glad to comply, he quickly lifted the chain from its shelter and circled her neck with the delicate string of gold. As he slipped the loop over the fastener, his lips brushed the back of her neck, causing a wave of warmth to course up and down her spine. His arms closed around her body, her back resting against his chest, his hands cupping her breasts.

"Will you meet me in Beaumont?"

He still hadn't said the words that Francyne wanted to hear, but as her fingertips brushed across the smooth gold knot in the center of her chain, she was contented. What he couldn't say in words, he had said with his gift. It wouldn't be long, she thought in her blissful ignorance, before he would say the words she wanted to hear.

"I will," she whispered, no hesitancy, thrilled as his warm lips traversed the sensitive area on the back of her neck, nipping a moist path below the chain.

"I have a small farm about a two hours' drive from Beaumont. We'll have the entire weekend to ourselves, and longer if you can stay."

Francyne's blood was pounding in her head, and she trembled in his arms. She could hardly contain her happiness. She leaned back against the muscular strength of his body, and his lips found their way to the arched column of her throat.

"We won't be bothered with family dropping in or with Keeley ruining our evenings."

Breathlessly Francyne chuckled, "It wasn't all that bad, was it?"

"Bad enough," he countered dryly, spinning her around. "Between your mother and Keeley my courting style has undergone a drastic change, one that I'm not too pleased about at all." He chuckled, his mouth brushing against the satiny smoothness of her cheek. "This is the first time I've had to abduct my woman in order to be alone with her, and it's the first time I've ever invited a woman to my little sanctuary."

Francyne's mind, like that of any woman in love, caught and held onto a few key words, incorrectly overreacting to them, misinterpreting the real meaning of what he had said. Over and over she sang the words *my woman*. She basked in the joy of his confession that she was the first woman he'd invited to his country home.

"What's it like?" she asked shyly.

"Just wait and see," he said. "I'll take you on a guided tour and let you see for yourself."

His lips captured hers in another long and satisfying kiss, and his moist mouth crushed down on hers, his tongue sweeping grandly into the musky cavern. Finally he reluctantly tore himself away from her, and sat up on the bed, running his hands through his tossled hair. He looked at the clock that was busily ticking away the passing minutes.

"I've got to go, sweetheart." He smiled sadly. "I don't want to, but I have to."

Francyne could hear the reluctance in his voice, and she smiled, sitting up in the middle of the bed. She watched him as he walked to the dresser and picked up her comb, raking it through his hair. She watched as he buttoned his shirt, straightened his tie, and slipped into his jacket.

He returned to the side of the bed and stood, looking down into her upturned face. His brown eyes penetrated the gateway to her soul—those elusive, ever-varying eyes that he loved so much. When he saw the raw want and desire that flamed in them, his fingers touched her face. With that promise he could wait for the coming weekend.

CHAPTER SIX

Brendan, dressed in a hunter-green vee-necked pullover and designer jeans, waited impatiently in the arrival lounge of the airport. He watched as the passengers slowly disembarked. Finally he spotted Francyne, his lips automatically twitched into a smile, and he exhaled a soft sigh of relief. He hadn't allowed himself to believe she would really come until he saw her in person.

He walked closer to the door and stood watching as she walked across the asphalt, carrying her small overnight case. He thought she was one of the most stunning women that he'd ever known, not the most beautiful, but the most fascinating. And each time that he saw her, he saw a different facet of her personality. As usual, he noted, she was dressed for the occasion.

Her hair was combed into a sleek chignon that rested elegantly against the nape of her neck. Her neck looked long and slender, adorned by the gold chain, which was exposed by the scoop neck of her dark brown blouse. Her off-white skirt, straight and slit in the front, was complemented by her matching linen blazer and her brown high-heeled sandals.

As she walked through the doors into the terminal Brendan met her, taking the overnight case with one hand and plucking her sunglasses off with the other. When he had looked into her golden-brown eyes, he planted a brief kiss on her lightly glossed lips.

He said in an undertone, "That's your greeting for now. I'll save the rest for later."

Francyne laughed and her cheeks blushed crimson. She tucked her hand into the crook of his arm, and the two of them sauntered down the corridor to the luggage area to get her other suitcases.

"How long can you stay?" Brendan asked as he handed her the small case and lifted up the two larger ones. "Through next week?"

Francyne nodded her head. "Berta returned to work today and insisted that I take next week off." She smiled. "She's all for romance. While she was in Mexico she met a dashing man who's sweeping her off her feet, and at the moment she's rather mellow."

"For my sake, I'm glad," Brendan returned lightly, leading the way out of the building, across the parking lot, to the car that he had rented.

"My, my," Francyne teased when she saw the large, sleek car, "this is different from your sports job."

He laughed. "Keeping up the businessman's image. Driving the conservative luxury car." He threw her cases into the trunk and slammed the lid. "You don't like it?"

"Much better," she replied, "at least the two of us can sit close to each other in the front seat. You know, those bucket seats only allow for so much togetherness."

"You tired or hungry?" he asked, opening the door on the driver's side, letting her slide in.

She leaned her head against the sun-warmed upholstery and shook her head. "I'm not tired. Today was fairly easy, and with Berta back I wasn't overwhelmed with work." She laughed softly. "In fact, she gave me the afternoon off, so I've been lazing around, taking my time getting ready."

Not caring that they were sitting outside a busy terminal and that people were strolling by periodically, Brendan slipped in beside her, narrowing the distance between them, putting his arms around her. With imperceptible pressure he drew her toward him so that she was lying against his torso. Slowly he rubbed his hands up and down her back. Finally he tired of the thick barrier of material between them and slipped his hands under her jacket. He softly spoke, his lips against her hair, his breath tantalizing on her cheeks.

"Has anyone ever told you how desirable you are, Francyne LaRue?"

"Not too many," she admitted truthfully, her face moving up and down against the cushiony softness of the green shirt. She chuckled. "I've never allowed myself to get close enough to a man for him to tell me." She lifted her eyes and flashed their impudence into his.

He chuckled deeply. "I see that I'm going to have my hands full training you."

"You can try," she replied in the same spirit, "but I don't think you'll succeed. You know the old cliché, you can't teach an old dog new tricks."

"I don't believe in worn-out clichés," he retorted, "and even if I did, I can't quite picture you as an old dog." He grinned. His lips were close to hers, almost touching. "Have you ever been close enough to a man

136

to let him kiss you and touch you like I have?" His voice was low and husky.

"I never kiss and tell."

He laughed deeply within his chest and drew her closer, his fingers cupping the base of her neck. Gently he pulled her head back, exposing the slender arch of her neck, looking at the shining chain around her neck. Slowly he brought his lips down to it, alternately nibbling and feathering kisses from the base of her throat to her ears.

She inhaled sharply, giddy with these sensations that only Brendan could arouse in her, happily giving herself up to complete abandon, feeling no qualms at the moment. She lifted her arms and wrapped them around his neck and shoulders, her fingers seeking that familiar terrain of hard muscle.

Now he lowered his lips to hers, kissing her softly and tenderly, not asking for admission into her mouth, just savoring the delectable fullness of her lips. His embrace was still loose, his hands still caressing her back, his passion well in check. He didn't want to flood her with a torrent of emotion that she couldn't handle, nor did he want to become too aroused at the moment himself. This was neither the time nor the place.

Finally his lips withdrew and he murmured into her ear, "Just how did you manage to get away from the family for the weekend, to say nothing of next week?"

Indignantly Francyne pulled out of his arms and glared at him. "The way you say *the family* makes them sound like they're part of the criminal underworld."

Brendan chuckled. "That's not quite what I meant, honey, but you've got to admit they've been ganging up on me ever since I've been seeing you."

Francyne laughed with him. "That's just your imagination, because you've been having bad thoughts."

He groaned, conceding the accuracy of her assertion. "You're right, Franny, I've just been having them, and the thought is killing me. I've always been a man of few words and a lot of action." He grinned into her face, momentarily forgetting his question. "I'm learning patience from you, if nothing else."

Francyne chuckled, watching as he slid under the wheel and started the engine. Settling back to enjoy the ride, she listened to the pleasant lilt of Brendan's voice as he conversed about many different subjects, conversation that was designed to be entertaining as well as informative, designed to put her totally at ease before they reached his farm.

"What made you buy a farm in Texas when you lived in Louisiana?" she asked curiously.

Brendan shrugged. "We were cutting timber in this area several years ago, and the farm was up for sale. The house was pretty quaint, and I liked it. I had enough saved up for a good-sized downpayment, so I bought it."

"Doesn't it bother you to leave it empty for long periods of time?"

"I don't. When I'm not here, a very close friend of mine stays in the house. A woman I've known for a long time."

"Oh?" Francyne raised her eyebrows.

He laughed, a rich mellow sound. "Caroline Weaver. She's one of the permanent women in my life and one of my favorites."

"And what is this favorite lady of your life like?" Just the right amount of indignation was injected into the question.

"Older, more experienced than you," he returned airily, enjoying his subterfuge. "To be truthful," he added, "she's really a terrific gal."

"Just how much older?" Francyne demanded, wondering if this was a game they were playing or not.

"I'd say about"—he paused as if thinking—"about eighty, but I can't be sure. She won't tell her age." When he glanced at Francyne, his eyes were twinkling.

"She'd better be," Francyne replied quietly in an amused undertone. "Now tell me why she's one of your favorite women."

And he did. For the next two hours or more they talked while Brendan drove through the verdant beauty of the East Texas countryside, finally turning onto a narrow dirt road.

"When you said country, you meant country!" Francyne exclaimed, drinking in the lush Big Thicket landscape, her eyes scaling the tall, stately pine trees that seemed to disappear into the clouds.

Brendan smiled. "It's a different kind of beauty from San Antonio, and it's one that I identify with more readily." He shrugged, smiling apologetically at her frown of disapproval. "I guess it's because I was raised in this neck of the woods, as the old-timers say."

He slowed the car, braking gently, pointing through the windshield to the clearing ahead. "Look ahead, Francyne! There's the house." He paused, then said, "That's my sanctuary—the place where I come to hide every once in a while to preserve my sanity."

Francyne didn't know what she expected, but certainly not the humble country cottage that was nestled beneath the majestic green canopy of the trees.

"It's beautiful," she breathed, seeing beyond the frame house, seeing into the soul of the man who was sitting beside her.

Her glance took in the dogwood tree, covered with beautiful green foliage, and the expansive chinaberry tree in its deep hunter-green. Across the dirt road that ran in front of the house was a host of pink honeysuckles, the aroma wafting toward them on the gentle breeze. On the weather-worn picket fence honeysuckle vines grew in profusion.

She turned to face him; their lips almost touched, they were sitting so close. "It's beautiful, Brendan," she sighed. "Really beautiful."

He stopped the car, turned off the ignition, and pulled the key out. "It—" He swiveled on the seat, wanting to look directly into her eyes as he spoke. Again he raised a hand and eased her glasses off her face. "I don't want you to misunderstand what I'm about to say," he began softly. "I mean it as a compliment."

Francyne nodded, swallowing that lump that formed so frequently in her throat when she and Brendan were together; she wondered what he was about to confess. She delighted in the rapture she felt when he bared a little more of his soul to her.

"None of my family knows about it." The frankness of his expression touched Francyne's heart. "But that's not what I want to tell you." He smiled, his secret making his eyes shine. "And I know this is going to seem totally out of character for me—"

Francyne glanced from his face to the house, then back to him. Being in love with the man and having glimpsed his soul, though for only a moment, she knew that the house was in character for him. But of course loved blinded . . . She stopped short. Or had love opened her eyes? Had love opened her eyes to what Brendan really was and what he really wanted out of life?

"I've never invited anyone out here before." He paused, his eyes frankly penetrating into hers.

She nodded, understanding what he wasn't saying,

140

listening tolerantly to what he was. "It's really beautiful, Brendan, and I mean it. I love the house." And I love you.

He touched her without touching her when he saw the reflection of her silent declaration. His eyes caressed her with their burning warmth, sending liquid heat through her bones, melting their rigidity, melding him and Francyne together into one being. Of course, being unschooled in the concept of love, Brendan didn't know what he was doing. Perhaps if he had known, he would have turned the car around right at that moment and would have driven Francyne into town to stay at a motel during her visit. He would have concentrated on the pleasures of sex rather than on molding and shaping a priceless love. But he wasn't consciously aware of what he was doing.

"It's more beautiful now," Brendan said, walking into the spell that he had so carefully woven, becoming entangled in its mystic web, guiding Francyne with him, both lost in the magic of the moment.

He reached out with one finger—just one finger—and lightly touched her cheek, tracing her jawline. Francyne's lips quivered from the rush of emotions that clamored through her body, and they parted, wanting the hot moistness of his, hungry and thirsty for his touch. Still he remained motionless.

"When I met you," he confessed in a low, velvety tone, "you reminded me of this house."

The finger feathered across her parted lips. She sat motionless, shivers of delight racing through her. Her breath was shallow and quick.

"You're unusual; you're real." His face was somber, no levity in his eyes, no teasing grin on his lips. "Like my house, you're unique." He saw the understanding in her eyes. "That's why I brought you here. That's why I waited. This was the right place for you and me."

Her eyes, a golden brown, almost the color of her hair, reflected the deep brown of her silk blouse, and tears caused them to shimmer like cut diamonds. She could only nod. She had no control over her tongue, over her emotions, over her love.

She was glad she had bought him the matching chain. At the right moment she would give it to him, and he would understand: he would recognize his love for her. It would look beautiful on his muscular neck, nestled in that crisp, wiry hair.

Now his hand cupped her chin, his fingers brushing seductively against her cheeks. "I've never brought another woman up here, because they didn't fit my house." His eyes smiled into hers, and the other hand gently pulled on her hands. "You're the first to share this haven with me."

His honesty had disarmed Francyne totally. She wasn't aware that he was inching closer, that she was inching closer. She only knew she must touch him as he had touched her. She yearned for him and would not stand being separated any longer.

"Perhaps we'll change it from a haven into a heaven," he intoned softly, his lips moving against hers.

"Perhaps," she agreed.

His lips nipped at the warm fullness of hers, teasing, whetting her desires. Then she tired of his game. Her hands capped the back of his head, and her lips, hot and moist, found his. She first nibbled the full hardness of his, sampling their richness, tantalizing him as he had tantalized her. Then her tongue stroked out, asking admittance into the mysterious depth of his mouth, and as her hand tangled in the black curls and her fingertips made the nerve endings tingle in his scalp, his mouth opened.

When the kiss finally ended, he murmured huskily, "Are you ready to go in?"

She nodded, and his arms closed around her in comforting warmth, all erotic overtones slowly dissipating. Brendan sat very still, quelling the riotous desires that stampeded through his body. He had waited too long for this moment; he had worked too hard for this reward. He refused to let his impatience mar its beauty. But again it was hard for him to keep his hands off her. He wanted her with a gut-want that was painful.

One hand gently tapped her chin, guiding her face upward, and his lips moved down to the naked skin above the scoop neck of the blouse. They brushed tormentingly around the base of her neck, his tongue stroking the fine mesh of gold that circled it.

"I thought we were going in," Francyne managed on a wobbly gasp.

Brendan chuckled softly. "I suppose we will if I can keep my hands off you long enough." Then he looked around, peering back in both directions. When his eyes came back to her face, they were filled with impish glints. "I almost expect Keeley or your mother to drop in on us by parachute at any minute."

Jarred suddenly from the heights of ecstasy, she pushed out of his arms and exclaimed over a smothered chuckle, "You're exaggerating, Brendan O'Shea, and you know it." But the smile lingered in her eyes and on her lips.

He grinned, conceding defeat. "A little perhaps, but not much." He opened the car door and slid across the seat, swinging his legs out. Then he remembered. "I would like to know what you told your mother."

Francyne wanted to evade the question as she'd done

earlier, so she said nothing. Brendan persisted this time. He leaned over, grabbed her hand, and tugged her across the seat.

"What did you say to her?"

Francyne smiled slowly. "I told her the truth." Brendan's brows arched doubtfully. Francyne's smile turned into a grin. "I told her I was spending the weekend with a friend."

Brendan nodded his head. "I see," and he clearly did. "And she didn't bombard you with questions?"

How well Brendan understood Sylvia LaRue! She shook her head. "No, she didn't." Quietly, in a small, subdued voice Francyne added, "She knew."

And didn't approve, Brendan exclaimed silently, watching the wistful expression that had settled on Francyne's face. Wisely he let the subject drop, wondering why he'd insisted on resurrecting it in the first place. He certainly didn't want Francyne tormenting herself with any more recriminations and guilt feelings. And he knew her well enough to know that if she thought about her mother's disapproval of premarital sex for long, she would feel guilty. And he didn't want that! Not at all!

He dropped her hands and walked to the back of the car, where he unlocked the trunk and lifted out the suitcases. "Here," he said, handing her the small overnight bag, "you can carry this one, and I'll take the rest. Or would you prefer to be liberated and carry the two heavier ones while I carry the small one?"

"Don't be cute," she retorted dryly. "You're too old and too big for that."

Laughing, they walked up the stone pathway to the porch, Brendan again talking casually about the house, easing the tension that he had created with his foolish blunder. He led the way into the bedroom and set her suitcases on the antique chest beneath the window.

As if drawn by a magnetic force, Francyne's eyes darted to the bed with its off-white coverlet and the patchwork quilt that was folded across the foot. When her intimate thoughts—thoughts of her and Brendan holding each other on the bed—brought a warm flush to her face, she quickly averted her eyes, looking first at the dresser, next at the chest of drawers, then at the large platform rocker. The intimacy of the room oppressed her; she wasn't ready for it yet.

Preoccupied with introducing Francyne to the room, Brendan hadn't noticed her meticulous inspection, and wasn't aware at all of her nervousness.

"This side of the dresser is yours." His hand swept down the length of the massive piece before he walked across the room and opened the door of the large wardrobe. "And you can hang your clothes in here."

"This room," Francyne began on a squeak, her first two fingers swinging around the chain at her throat. She cleared her throat and tried again. "Your bedroom is pretty. Did you decorate it yourself?"

He noticed her apprehension, frowned inwardly, but didn't respond to it. "Yes," he replied, adjusting the blinds and the drapes, letting the evening sun filter softly into the room. "I hired an interior decorator, but she wanted to turn it into a chic monstrosity instead of trying to keep it in harmony with its surroundings. So I took over and created my own little world. Totally modern," he said, his hand gesturing around the room, indicating all the contemporary furnishings, which still had an unmistakably country flavor, "but totally comfortable and utilitarian." Then he laughed as he remembered something. "Well, it's almost all modern," he amended with a twinkle in his eyes. He reached for her hand. "Come with me, and I'll show you the bathroom."

Francyne had no choice but to follow, since he didn't let go of her hand. They walked through the living room, the dining room, and the kitchen to a large back porch. Brendan approached a closed door, and his hand clasped the knob.

"The house was built before they had indoor plumbing in this area," he explained, swinging the door open, motioning Francyne to step in. "So when the bathroom was installed, it was put out here."

Francyne gaped in amazement at the room, which was decorated in blacks, burgundies, and deep pinks. She was fascinated with its elegance and enthralled with its turn-of-the-century look.

"Brendan," she breathed, looking at the facsimile bathroom fixtures, the commode with the water reservoir mounted high on the wall with an ornate pull chain hanging down, the large four-legged, clawfoot bathtub, the wash basin with the antique mirror hanging above it, and the oil lamps that were mounted on the wall. "It's gorgeous." She turned to him. "I didn't know you liked the old-timey look."

"I don't necessarily," Brendan said. "This is what the decorator did. Every time I take a bath, I feel like I'm on display. I sorta expect cameramen to zoom in. You know, it looks like a set for a movie." He walked over to the burgundy drapes that covered one wall. "I compromised," he said, pulling the drawstring, revealing an ultramodern recessed shower stall. "I let the antique look stay, so long as I could have a shower installed. Taking a bath in that four-legged monster isn't my idea of fun."

Francyne laughed, imagining his large frame wedged

146

into the old-fashioned bathtub. "I still like it," she said. "It looks so romantic."

Brendan let go of the drawstring and moved closer to Francyne. "Perhaps it can be romantic. Shall we find out?"

Francyne laughed again, and Brendan could detect the nervous overtones. "I don't think so," she replied evenly, her hands running up and down the lapels of her coat. "Not right now, anyway."

Don't move too fast, he advised himself, stepping back, smiling directly at her. He turned his wrist and looked at his watch. Abruptly and totally changing the subject, he asked, "Did you get anything to eat on the plane?"

Francyne, glad he had abandoned the provocative topic of their taking a bath together, quickly responded in an overly loud voice. "They served food, but I wasn't hungry."

Food hadn't been a primary concern of hers during the past week. She had existed on her growing excitement, on the thought of spending the weekend with Brendan. Today had been no exception. She had spent all afternoon getting ready, packing her new clothes, buying that expensive perfume, and getting her hair done.

"Well, then," Brendan declared, "I guess I'll have to feed you." He threw his arm loosely across her shoulders and guided her out of the bathroom. "Come with me," he said, "and see what I've prepared for you."

Not knowing what to expect next, Francyne looked at him, puzzlement reflected on her face. Amused by her reaction, Brendan laughed, leading the way into the kitchen, which had been stripped and modernized yet hadn't lost any of its country charm. He walked to the refrigerator and began to rummage around, lifting out several dishes, one of which was a large casserole.

Setting it on the table, he pronounced proudly, "Now I don't make any claim to culinary fame, and I can't turn out any of those LaRue specialties, but I can make one fantastic tuna-and-noodle casserole." He walked into the pantry and came out with a jar of instant tea. "I haven't mastered the instant tea bit, but I have other plans for tonight." His eyes twinkled. "I figure that a lady deserves a little champagne on her twenty-eighth birthday, don't you?"

Nodding her head, Francyne began to laugh softly, not so much at Brendan's antics as from the excitement that was building up inside her. She could feel the tiny stream as it burgeoned into a river, ready to overflow its banks. She wet her lips with the tip of her tongue.

"Mind if I change before we eat?"

Brendan shook his head.

"I'll hurry so I can help you."

"No rush," Brendan replied. "There's not much to getting it ready." He grinned. "I'm quite undomesticated."

Francyne shyly smiled at him and disappeared into the master bedroom. At the same time he went from the pantry to the refrigerator to the cupboard, taking out the cheese, the crackers, the cutting board, and the cutlery. He loaded the tray and carried the food into the living room, setting it on the coffee table.

Looking around the room, liking the large white throw rug even more, he threw several colored pillows on top of it. Innocently seductive, he thought, admiring his strategy. Then he walked over to the stereo, letting the soft music flow through the room, and he turned the lamps down low so that the dim light filtered through the room, adding the final touch to the sensuous scene.

He made his last trip to the kitchen and was just clicking out the light when Francyne stepped out of the bedroom. Standing still in the door frame, Brendan was holding a bottle of his favorite vintage in one hand, chilled and ready to serve, and in the other he held two crystal glasses. His brown eyes raked over the woman standing by the coffee table.

"You're lovely," he breathed, finally taking the steps that brought him close to her. "That orange fabric—" He didn't complete his sentence. He just drank in the beauty of her appearance, the polyester crepe that draped over her curves, totally covering her but creating a uniquely sensual illusion. He couldn't get over the way she used clothes to her best advantage—he could visualize every inch of the satin carpet of skin beneath the delicate fabric.

His brown eyes swept upward again, resting on her flushed face. He held both hands up. "Champagne?"

Nervously she nodded her head and unconsciously wiped her hands down the seam of the pants. "Okay."

Brendan nodded and with a grand flourish indicated that she should sit down in front of the coffee table. "This will be more comfortable than the dining table or the kitchen table," he informed her, kneeling down himself to pour out two glasses of champagne.

Francyne glanced around, totally seduced by the setting. She eased her shoes off her feet, curled her legs under her, and took the glass that Brendan handed her. When he raised his to his lips, she watched, holding her glass in her hand.

He set his glass down on the coffee table and followed Francyne's example. He took his shoes off; then he lifted his glass again, sipping slowly, watching her over

149

the rim. She still hadn't tasted hers. He wondered why. Did she think he was trying to get her drunk?

Surely not, he thought. That was the farthest thing from his mind. Sure, he wanted her relaxed and responsive to his advances, but he didn't want her drunk. He wanted her to be fully aware of everything they did. But at the same time he was in no mood for a sparring match between Francyne and her conscience. So he set out to woo her, to court her, and to consummate their courtship.

As if she had read his mind and agreed with him, Francyne slowly raised her glass and sipped the effervescent liquid, the bubbles tickling her nose. Then Brendan reached out, took her glass from her fingers, and touched his lips to the spot where hers had rested. He handed his glass to her, and he watched.

Hypnotized by the sheer intimacy of this act, Francyne did not have the will to deny him. Without taking her eyes from his face, she lifted the glass and put her lips where his had been. She could feel the warmth of his mouth on hers, and she could feel the warmth of his passion as it flowed down her throat, burning every inch of her.

Brendan set the glass down, picked up a cracker, broke it, and dipped it into the casserole. Then he carried it to her mouth.

"Open wide," he commanded softly, and he inserted the morsel into her mouth.

They fed each other, laughing and talking, enjoying and savoring each other's presence, glad of the opportunity to be alone with their questing as each discovered the bare, essential truth of the other. Not once did they entertain the idea that they needed more; they were content with the world they were creating.

Sometimes during the evening, they moved the coffee

table, and they sprawled on the rug, not together, but close, their heads on the throw pillows, side by side, talking, sharing more secrets about themselves. Brendan suddenly rolled on his side, propped himself on one arm, and stared into her face.

"This hardwood floor is very hard."

His finger touched her lips and when he withdrew it, her tongue darted out, licking them, and he watched as it peeked out and returned once again to the moistness of her mouth. He accepted the invitation, his lips drawing closer until they brushed lightly against hers in a teasing gesture. Not stopping in their quest, they moved lower, touching the cherished lover's knot that lay in the hollow of Francyne's throat. They moved lower still until they touched the fabric that stretched taut over her breasts.

Touching the peak, he blew his warm breath through the material, his fingers moving up under the top to fan out against her naked stomach. Her body convulsed with longing, and her hand covered his, pressing his fingers into her flesh, and she turned her head back and forth on the pillow as her nipples hardened.

"I've waited so long for you," he whispered.

"Not really," she replied, her eyes glazed with passion.

"I feel like it's been an eternity." His brown eyes were filled with her image. "Are you ready for bed?"

She nodded, not moving, marveling at the thrill of knowing that at the moment she was the center of his thoughts, the axis of his world. At the moment everything he did or said revolved around her.

"Do you want me to undress you?"

She smiled, composed, almost serene. "No, I'd like for you to give me a few minutes."

He nodded and sprang to his feet, stretching out a

hand to help her up. "I'll clean up the mess while you change." On a lighter note he added, "Tonight is your night, my lady. I'll accede to your every wish."

Francyne smiled, no nervous twitters now. She took a few steps across the room and turned to stare at the man who stooped over the coffee table, gathering up the remains of their feast. He raised his face, and they stared at one another.

Francyne could read the longing and desire in his eyes. They begged her to hurry. They told her that he wanted to hold her, to love her, to make her his. The thoughts were sweetly caressing, and they brought a lovely flush to her face. She automatically brought her other hand up and touched her rose-tinted cheek. Tonight she would know Brendan more intimately than she'd ever known any other man.

This intimacy was more than having sex with a man; it was more than sleeping with a man. It was the knowledge gained from having loved a man, having learned to know the inner man. She would learn about his secret self as he would learn about her. They would share things in their loving that they would not otherwise have shared.

Her fingers dropped down her cheek, coming to rest on that precious gold chain that coiled so snugly against her lower throat. She felt the thickness and the oneness of the knot—the lover's knot—and her stomach began to churn. She didn't know how much more of her love she could shut up inside her. A fire was burning deep inside, and soon the flames would burst out.

Brendan, his hands full of dishes, forced himself to remain where he was. He wouldn't let anything, not even a wrong move by himself, mar the beauty of the moment. Before his eyes he was seeing Francyne become his woman. He could see the mental transformation as it took place; he could feel it.

He could hardly wait for the moment that he took her to be his, to fully claim her, to usher her into realms, realms of . . . love. The word was alien to his thoughts, but it was the only one that fit. He'd take her to realms of love that she'd never known before. The uniqueness of the moment, the caring, the almost-loving shone in Brendan's eyes, giving Francyne a glimpse of his vulnerability, his sensitivity.

She turned and walked into the bedroom, softly closing the door behind her. She turned on the lamp beside the bed, and a dim light filled the room. She stepped out of the lounge suit and hung it up. Then she unclasped her bra and pulled her panties off. She walked over to the dresser and pulled out the drawer where she'd put her new nightgown, the one she'd bought for this special night.

She held the ecru lace and shimmering silk above her head and let it glide downward. Then she brushed her hair, letting it hang in gilded waves over her shoulders and down her back. She gazed at herself in the shadowed mirror, wondering what Brendan's reaction would be. Even in the dim light she could see the shining gold of the lover's knot.

She pulled back the cover on the bed, then she turned off the lamp and walked to the window, standing in the silvery rays of moonlight that spilled into the room. Partly out of habit and partly in anticipation Francyne's hand ran across the ecru lace and up to the chain that she thought was Brendan's declaration of love. Patiently she waited.

Then she heard the door open and shut; she heard Brendan as he walked softly across the room. In the stillness of the spring evening she heard the rustle of fabric as he undressed in the near darkness behind her, but she didn't turn around. Then she felt him behind her.

His hands cupped her shoulders, and his face gently touched her skin, his lips adoringly, reverently planting kisses around the thin straps of her gown. The quivers of pleasure that ran through her caused her body to arch, to lean back against his, and her hands instinctively came up to press against her stomach.

She inhaled the familiar scent of him—musky, outdoorsy, and masculine. She smelled the champagne on his breath, sweet and tangy. She felt the cool, moist lips move over her shoulders, blazing a path through territory that hadn't been explored in a long time. The springy curls that covered his chest tickled her back, and she softly sighed her hunger for him.

His hands dropped from her shoulders to her breasts, cupping each one, pulling her more firmly against him. All the while his lips continued to nibble her neck, her earlobes, his tongue gently entering and swirling around the outer ear. She gasped in pleasure, trembling in his arms, her hands closing over each of his.

Then with a precision that neither thought about, that came naturally, he turned her in his arms, and she lifted her love-dazed face to his, her lips begging for the touch of his lips, her mouth hungry for the taste of his. Her eyes closed, the better to relish his touch, his presence, his scent. She moved closer, melding her softness into Brendan's solid frame.

His mouth possessed her, and she was enveloped by the flavor of him. A hidden artesian spring of desire . . . desire for Brendan O'Shea alone . . . welled up inside her, parting her lips, inviting and accepting the impulsive exploration of the deepening kiss, wanting the thrust of his tongue, seeking the hard pleasure of his body against hers.

Not sure when or how, he broke the kiss with a ragged groan and picked her up in his arms, carrying her to the bed. He laid his precious bundle of burning love on the bed. But Brendan was too involved in his seduction to realize that his inner vocabulary was subtly changing. He had never used such committable terms before. *Never!*

He stood beside the bed for the longest time, looking down at the woman, shimmering silver in the moonlight. Was she real? he wondered. Or was she some enchantress come to torment him, to weave a maddening spell of love around him and then disappear. Would she make love to him, make him love her, and then return to that river from which she came?

Francyne couldn't read his shadowed face, but she could see the rigidity of his body. She could feel the ardent desire that washed over him in waves, splashing onto herself. She raised her left hand, the one closest to Brendan, and her fingers lightly touched the thick, powerful leg, running from the knee up to the thigh on the outside, gradually moving toward the inside, higher and higher.

The slow caress was like the beginning of an avalanche; each successive tremor of his body preparing the cascade of passion that would soon bury them both alive. Her hand touched the taut muscles of his loins, and he could stand no more. He collapsed on the bed beside her, clasping his hand to her hand, which still stroked and caressed his central him, guiding her in a fevered exploration of his surging masculinity, alerting her to his needs.

His lips caught and held hers, pilfering, plundering, and pillaging. Their lovemaking was reaching the stage of naked need and desire, leaving the delicacies and niceties of courtship far behind. Her hands were on his naked body as much as his hands were on hers. Both were learning, discovering, finding, and delighting in the feel of one another. Again and again their lips, his and hers, ravished the other's, breaking down barriers and inhibitions, making restitution for their long fast, the long denial.

When both were breathing quickly and heavily, when both were trembling, almost to the point of not being able to hold back any longer, he eased her from his arms and lifted her up. His fist closed over the filmy material of her gown, and he pulled it over her head, throwing it down on the floor beside the bed.

His fingers lightly feathered across her stomach, and she sucked in her breath, causing the muscles to tighten. She smiled tremulously, returning the caress, letting her fingers play on the sensitive area around his navel, lower into the groin. Her boldness and his response filled her with elation, with a sense of growing power in her ability to arouse, to provoke, to please.

She looked directly into his face, encountering at close range his beautiful brown eyes, shadowed and barely discernible in the moonlight, but she knew they smoldered with passion and desire—she hoped with love. As she stared her lips parted, and he leaned over her, brushing his lips lightly against hers as his hand tenderly kneaded the firm breast, the erect nipple. Then worshipfully, adoringly his lips brushed the other breast as they journeyed over her body.

Against her stomach he whispered, "I'm going to make you mine. You're going to belong to me body and soul, Francyne LaRue."

Her fingers twined through his hair, and she kneaded his scalp as he rained hot, wet kisses on her breasts, her rib cage, her navel, her belly. She gasped with heated pleasure, turning and twisting her body, her lips parted, her tongue glazing her lips with seductive nectar.

"Even if you don't make love to me," she panted, doubling her hands into fists, closing on the soft curls, pulling his face up to hers, "I belong to you, Brendan." Tears coursed down her cheeks. "You've already possessed me. All that's left is the coming together. I'm yours." Her voice dropped to an agonizing hoarseness. "For better or worse, I'm yours."

"For better, sweetheart, for better!" He savagely hissed the words as his lips claimed hers in that final assault, as his hand carefully prepared her for entry. He lovingly moved over her, and lowered himself into her welcoming softness.

She wrenched her mouth from his and her lips, pressed against the side of his face, made her confession.

"I love you, I love you, I . . ."

CHAPTER SEVEN

Home! she thought, standing in her bedroom, her hands resting on the empty night case that was still sitting on her dresser. Would she ever be home again? Would she ever have that comfortable, warm feeling again?

She moved lethargically to the window, pulling the drapes open, letting the warm sunshine spill into the room, wishing it could spill that easily into the darkness of her heart. She leaned her forehead on a windowpane, letting each hand rest on the frame. She had never dreamed a week ago, when she boarded the plane, that her week with Brendan would end like this.

She turned around, leaning her back against the window frame, gazing at her yellow linenlike suit, which she'd carefully set out on the bed. She looked at the crisp white blouse. Both were new. Meticulously chosen for her week with Brendan! How she'd plowed through her savings for those clothes! Now she didn't know if she'd ever wear them again.

Clad only in her underwear, she padded to the bed,

picked up the clothes, and headed toward the walk-in closet. Automatically she hung up her suit and blouse. No conscious thought was involved, merely reflexive action.

She stopped in front of the full-length mirror, and she studied her reflection. The face and the body were the same, but even she could detect a difference. Gone were the glowing eyes; gone was the trace of color that went with anticipation. In its place there was only a resigned sadness. The eyes, no longer elusive or changeable, had a definite dullness about them, almost a blankness.

Also gone was the gold chain that for a short period of time had been an integral part of Francyne LaRue's life. It lay abandoned, but not forgotten, in her jewelry box. She had tried to give it back to Brendan, but he had refused to take it. In her anger— no, she corrected herself, in her hurt and humiliation—she had jerked it from her neck, breaking the clasp, and had tossed it at his feet.

But when she had unpacked her suitcases, she had found it tucked into one of the side pockets. And even now, with all that had happened between them, she still loved it. It was her treasured possession. Even if it didn't speak of his love for her, it reminded her of her love for him.

Tears glistened in her eyes, and she walked to the bathroom, lifting the lid of the antique box that her grandmother had given her so many years ago. She lifted the tiny remembrance and let it dangle from her fingers. It was all she had left of Brendan besides her memories. It was her only tangible evidence that he had once been a part of her life.

The phone began ringing again. Dear Lord, she sighed, walking out of the bathroom, would it never stop? Ever since she'd returned from the lake house, it had been ringing almost constantly. She didn't think she could stand much more right now, and she'd ignored the loud piercing noise as long as she could. But she had no intention of talking with Brendan. Not now! Not ever!

Two, three, four rings! Purposefully she walked over to the obtrusive instrument, lifted the ivory receiver, and held it just above the cradle for a few minutes before she deliberately dropped it. She couldn't . . . no, better, she wouldn't take the chance of talking to him. She was too susceptible to his charm, to his arguments, to his reasoning. She couldn't think straight when she was around him.

Not bothering to dress, she walked into the kitchen and rummaged through the refrigerator and pantry. She didn't want to cook her supper, but neither did she want to go out. As she shoved the cans of food around, she found a can of chili. She turned her nose up in disdain, but she guessed it would do in a pinch, and this was a pinch.

She pulled open the cabinet door, got out a small saucepan, and set it on top of the stove. She glanced at the clock. Seven! She might drive to Sophie's after she'd eaten. Be good to see the brat again. That would definitely be better than sitting at home by herself. She opened the can, pouring the contents into the boiler. Then she opened a bag of Fritos, dumping some into the bottom of a bowl.

She wasn't in the mood to bother with making tea, so she opened a bottle of cola, splashing it over a glass full of ice. She smiled. This certainly wasn't what Sylvia LaRue would call a balanced meal, but it would keep her stomach from growling. By the time the chili was hot and ready to pour over the Fritos, she realized that the phone had finally stopped ringing. Good, she thought, dismissing it altogether.

She sat down at the small breakfast table and tentatively raised a spoonful of hot meat sauce and chips to her mouth, tasting it cautiously before taking the entire bite. Preoccupied with her disappointment and having no one to talk with, she devoted all her time to eating, and it wasn't long before she finished.

Quickly and efficiently she straightened up the kitchen and was walking to her bedroom when she heard the chime of the doorbell. She stopped moving, darting a furtive glance at the door. Brendan! It had to be him! Stupidly she had not reckoned on his getting here this soon. Really, Francyne, she thought, don't start lying to yourself!

Is this what she wanted? Yes! But now that he was here, she was scared. What next? What could they say that hadn't already been said! Fear and apprehension immediately chased all hope from her heart. She lifted her hand to her mouth, rubbing her lips with her clenched fingers. What should she do?

The insistent ringing of the doorbell had stopped. There was a moment of pregnant silence. Had he gone? Was she sorry? Was she relieved? Then came a loud pounding, followed by an authoritative voice.

"Francyne, I know you're in there, and I'm not leaving until you open this door."

He continued to pound on the door.

"Let me in."

"Just a minute," Francyne called when she had finally summoned up her courage. "I've got to get dressed."

"Hurry," he bellowed angrily. "I hate waiting outside in the hall like this."

But Francyne didn't hurry. Very slowly, spitefully, she walked to the bedroom, her mind whirling with conflicting emotions. *Joy.* He had cared enough to come see her. *Fear.* What if he didn't want any more from her today than he had wanted on the weekend? *Annoyance!* Why didn't he just leave her alone?

The doorbell, pealing three or four times consecutively, reminded her of the angry, impatient man on her doorstep. She scampered into the closet, dropping an old aqua tent dress over her shoulders, and the shoulders were about the only place that it fit. She giggled. Brendan would love this. Quickly she headed for the dresser, picked up the brush, and brushed her hair straight from her forehead, pulling it into a severe chignon on the crown of her head.

Brendan had begun to pound on the door!

Deliberately she picked up the white gold chain that Sterling had given her last year for Christmas, and she fumbled with the clasp. This would show Brendan O'-Shea. She'd let him know that she wasn't sitting around pining for him. There were other fish in the pond, her grandmother had said, and she'd show him that she'd been out fishing.

The pounding had increased in tempo, and she was afraid to dawdle any longer. She hurried to the door, unlocking the first lock. Brendan, hearing the click, twisted the knob, and opened the door a crack to glare at her.

"Hurry up," he thundered in ominous tones.

Nervously she fumbled with the night lock and chain. When she dropped her hands and stepped back, Brendan swept into the room like a hurricane in all its fury. Not frightened of him physically, but apprehensive about his reason for coming, leery of his anger, Francyne cautiously backed into the living room.

"I'm glad you could take time out of your busy evening to open the door," he shouted, his brown eyes

162

flashing angrily. "There's nothing I love any better than camping on someone's doorstep while she decides whether or not she's going to let me in."

His hand went to the collar of his immaculate white shirt, and he loosened the green-and-beige tie and the top button of his shirt. He walked into the room, stopping only when he had reached the sofa. Here he peeled off his beige jacket, deliberately folding it and laying it down on the back of the sofa. Then he calmly—or at least he gave the appearance of being calm—rolled his sleeves up a cuff or two.

Francyne, standing by the window now, interestedly watched his every move. Her eyes drank in the masculine presence, the devastating force that was unleashed in the room as soon as he walked in. She hungrily devoured him with her eyes. The strong hands and wrists that were revealed when he rolled up his shirt sleeves. The legs that stretched the fabric of his slacks when he walked.

He turned in the direction of the bar, crossing the dining area in two or three long strides. He looked at the different bottles, selected one, and set it aside. He walked into the kitchen, returning in a few minutes with a bucket of ice. As casually as if this were a chore he performed in her kitchen every day he dropped several cubes of ice into his glass and splashed scotch over the ice.

Now he turned and walked toward Francyne, without bothering to offer her a drink. He sat down in the chair that matched the sofa, kicked out his long legs, crossed them at the ankles, and stared at her over the rim of his glass. The brown eyes raked over her as she stood silhouetted against the window.

He couldn't tell what she was thinking. Not that she had on tinted glasses, she didn't. In fact, he thought, she wasn't wearing her glasses at all. That meant she couldn't really see him, not the details. All she could see was a fuzzy outline. This irritated him. He wanted her to see him, all of him.

He flicked his eyes from the top of her tightly pinned hair, to the bare feet, the toes that were digging into the pile of the carpet. Back up the eyes went, grimacing at the loose-fitting dress, stopping to glare at the silver-colored chain that hung around her neck.

His free hand balled into a fist, and he felt a wave of anger like he'd never felt before surging through his veins. If she wasn't going to wear his gift, he didn't want her wearing another man's. How did he know a man had given it to her? He just did! He had figured Francyne out, and she'd do it just to show him. Well, she'd shown him, and it hurt. God, he growled silently, it hurt.

He lowered the glass, having drained it of most of the liquor. "Where have you been?"

"Around" came the sharp answer, as if it were none of his business.

He glowered at her. "Where did you go after you left the farm?"

He never raised his voice, yet Francyne could have sworn that he had. The question was direct, emphatic, and forceful. Its tone implied that he would insist on an answer, an answer as direct and honest as the question.

Francyne turned her back to him, catching the flimsy curtain in her hands, running it between her fingers. She could be no less than honest with him. After all, she thought, he'd been honest with her. She smiled painfully, remembering. It was his honesty that had hurt so badly.

"When I took you to the airport, you said you were coming home."

She heard his words. She also heard the cool politeness that concealed the rising anger.

"No," she reminded him, "you said I was coming home." Her voice sounded as if she were the mistress of her emotions. "I had a full week of vacation left, and I didn't intend to waste it, so I went to stay with friends." This was inaccurate at best. She'd spent the remainder of the week with her grandparents in Tyler.

"You knew that I was coming back Tuesday," he accused softly, not moving from the chair. "I told you that I'd be here to see you and that we'd talk."

"I didn't say I'd be here." Still she didn't turn around. "Furthermore," she added, "I think we said all there was to be said. What more can we say? You're what you are, and I'm what I am." The echo of her voice had drifted into silence before she added, "If there's any more to say, it could only be because you have changed your way of thinking." He made no comment. Evidently he hadn't changed his mind. Well, she thought obstinately, she hadn't either.

She would never forget their last day together. How naive she had been. How stupid! How he must have laughed at her. She turned red with mortification just thinking about it.

She had awakened to a world of love, or so she had thought. Brendan was cuddled close to her, his legs nestling in the curve of hers, his arm draped over her body, their hands intertwined. She felt his warm breath blowing the hair that lay on her neck; then she felt one hand as it traveled from her breast down to her abdomen, resting there possessively.

"I can't get enough of you," he murmured in his sleep-thickened voice. "I want you all over again."

He turned over on his side and propped himself up on one arm, looking into her face, radiant with love.

He'd never seen this look before, and it frightened him. He had known that Francyne was different from the other women in his life, but he hadn't planned on her falling in love with him, had he? Perhaps he hadn't, he agreed, but he'd certainly known it and had taken advantage of it. He surely couldn't be accused of discouraging her.

You knew she would, his conscience nagged. You suspected it when you first met her, and you were certain of it when you gave her that necklace. Oh, I know, you didn't know what the necklace would mean to her, but you had studied her well enough to know that she wouldn't take such an expensive gift lightly. And remember the day you kissed her doubts away! The day you kissed the chain all around her throat. You used it as a tool for your own selfish motives.

"I want you too," she said, letting her slumbrous eyes fill up with the handsomeness of the man beside her.

He caught her left hand, which was curved above her head, and he held it; his body pinned down her right hand. His teeth caught the cover, pulling it down, exposing her breasts, pink and rosy, faint marks of love dotting the darker circlet around the nipple. Then his mouth feathered hot, wet kisses over the creamy mounds, his lips closing on first one, then the other nipple, loving them.

Francyne arched her back, squirming her buttocks, groaning in ecstasy. She moved her legs to the erotic rhythm Brendan was setting. Finally he stopped her frenzied movement by capturing her legs between his, and she could only toss her head back and forth in passionate abandon.

She fought until she had freed her left hand, lowering it until it rested on the crown of his black hair. She turned her face, nibbling hungrily, desperately at his chest, her mouth and tongue seeking the nipples that were hidden in the carpet of hair. Her hand slipped around his ribs and under his arm to gently trace teasing designs on his back while her tongue etched fiery paths around his chest, causing the nipples to harden.

She began to slide down, just so much, letting her lips and her tongue move along the hard, flat plane of his stomach, her hand smoothing and soothing to his side and buttocks. As she nibbled the moist kisses on his diaphragm, around his navel, her hand kneaded the flexed hardness of his thighs, and she half-turned, pulling him closer to her, thrilling herself as he pressed his maleness into her feminine softness.

Again he carried her to that mountain of passionate repletion, that lovely oneness that is shared only by lovers. They smelled the fragrance of the erotic flowers of passion; they drank at the crystal clear river of desire, they explored all the wonders of each other, then stood at the summit and stared at the sweet valley of completeness below.

Slowly they walked, or they floated, or they glided . . . they weren't sure . . . toward the valley, their physical bodies and their souls united, their minds as one. Francyne had never known such blinding sensations, had never known that love meant so much giving. With no regard for herself she gave, freely and completely, gave before she thought of receiving.

Brendan, if he had analyzed his feelings, would have been compelled to admit that he, too, had given. He wanted Francyne's pleasure before his own, her hunger abated, her thirst slaked; then he had reveled in her goodness and her giving, which flowed so freely. He had been one with her, in her, and for her. But Brendan didn't analyze his feelings; he wasn't ready for the truth yet.

Afterward, as they lay together in bed, enjoying the aftermath of their love, basking in the glory of the moment, Brendan had said, "Happy birthday, sweetheart." And he had kissed the chain around her neck, beginning at the right collar bone, moving around to the left, his lips stopping at the gold knot.

Francyne's happiness was overflowing, and she couldn't help but believe that Brendan felt the same for her as she felt for him. She smoothed her fingers through the back of his hair, murmuring to him, planting sweet kisses on the crown of his head.

"Thank you for this birthday, my darling," she said softly. "It's been the most wonderful one I've ever had." She caught his face in her hands and guided it upward. She looked into his eyes. "I love you."

The confession was soft, but Brendan could feel the depth of meaning. He could hardly stand to look into her eyes, to see the awesome wonder of love, the glowing radiance and beauty of her womanhood fulfilled. She didn't notice his reluctance, however, because she was too caught up in her own joy. She jumped up from the bed, and, quite naked, she ran to find her purse, which was lying on the antique chest beneath the window. She opened it and pulled out the jeweler's box.

She proudly walked back to the bed, watching the passion that stirred in Brendan's eyes. Her body tingled warmly from the flames that so suddenly seemed to leap to life. She reveled in her prowess as a woman, capable of stirring a man's senses like this. She was thankful that she'd met and fallen in love with Brendan. She handed him the box.

"Something special for you," she whispered.

He picked the box up and turned it over in his hands

several times. Cautiously he opened it; his mind had seized on the words "something special." He stared at the gold chain; he was pleased with the selection, but he wasn't pleased with the gift. He knew that Francyne wouldn't give him an expensive gift like this unless . . .

"Do you like it?" she asked softly, her eyes searching his face for some sign of pleasure and recognition.

He nodded his head, not knowing what to say next. "It's beautiful," he said, slowly taking the chain out of the box, letting it dangle from one of his extended fingers. "Thank you." But he didn't recognize the tiny lover's knot that rested in the center of the gold thread.

Francyne smiled tentatively, her lips trembling slightly with disappointment. She couldn't know that Brendan had never really noticed the chain that he had given her, and thus he hadn't recognized its mate. She tried again after this lackadaisical reaction.

"Are you going to put it on?"

"Of course." He grinned, wondering why he had been so remiss. The gift had shaken him up so much that he wasn't thinking clearly. How was he to handle things now?

He scooted over to the edge of the bed, turning his back to her. "Unclasp this one for me, will you? Then you can put yours around my neck."

"Do you really like it?" she asked again, probing for the right answer.

"Of course I do, sweetheart," he answered, his voice impatient. "How many times must I tell you? Now be a good girl and hook it for me."

Francyne's face underwent an immediate change. The lovely glow faded, and a sad, haunted melancholy filled her eyes. At the time she wouldn't have admitted it, but she knew that Brendan didn't love her. She backed away from the bed and went to get her robe, which was lying the chest where her purse had been. She moved awkwardly; without the garment of love she was all too aware of her nakedness.

Suddenly the warmth fled from the room, and she felt a chill. She crossed her arms on her chest, and she looked around the room. She couldn't look at him, or she would have burst into tears. And she waited. She waited for him to say something about the chain. She prayed that he would.

Aware of Francyne's withdrawal Brendan had no idea what had happened. It had something to do with the gift, he knew. But beyond that, he wasn't sure. He could tell that she had expected a different reaction; she expected more from him than he had given. Still he didn't know what.

Well versed in subtleties of this kind, Brendan knew that he had erred. But, he thought, hadn't he said the right words at the right moment? Certainly he hadn't been any too swift, but he had suggested that she put it around his neck. What more did he want?

Giving jewelry to women had always been part of the game. He'd never really thought of it as much more than that, and when the woman had given him a gift, he had accepted it in the same spirit. He should have remembered that Francyne was different; she was so sensitive, so emotional. She still let her heart rule rather than her head.

By now she was standing in front of the window, facing him. "Did you notice anything in particular about the chain?" She sounded as if she were calm and composed. "Does it remind you of anything?"

Completely in the dark, Brendan shook his head. "Is it supposed to remind me of something?" Dear God, he breathed, what had he missed?

"You don't recognize it?" Tears wavered in her voice, but she wasn't about to lose control.

What was wrong with him? she wondered. Why was he acting so peculiar about the chain? He had been with her. He had heard the saleswoman. Wasn't that his reason for having bought the necklace? Wasn't it the special gift that he'd bought for her? Wasn't she someone special in his life?

He scooted off the bed, unmindful of his nakedness, and walked to the full-length mirror that covered the door of the wardrobe. He studied the chain that hung around his neck; he ran his fingers over it once or twice. He walked over to where Francyne was standing, and he unzipped her robe just far enough to reveal her chain.

"Dear God," he muttered, his voice empty of all expression, "you bought me the matching chain."

Nothing, Francyne thought. He felt nothing. Miserably she stood and watched as he padded over to the bed, slipped into his shorts and jeans, and moved around the room. The silence lengthened; the tension heightened.

For once in his life Brendan didn't know how to handle the situation, and it was volatile, to say the least. The wrong word and Francyne would blow up. Already she was on the verge of exploding. Yet he still didn't know the right words to say.

He racked his brain, trying to remember, going back to the day when he bought her the necklace. What had that woman been telling Francyne? What was it that the necklace was supposed to mean? Evidently it was very important to her. Something so important that his reaction had upset her this much.

He walked over to where Francyne was standing; he caught both her hands in his and looked into her face. She was too important to him. He couldn't afford to

171

lose her because he hadn't been paying attention and didn't remember the significance of the chain. At the same time she was too important for him to lie.

"I really love the chain," he said. "Thank you very much." Even he had to admit the words sounded very prosaic.

Francyne knew now; there was no doubt. Brendan didn't understand. She withdrew her hands from his clasp. "It's all right," she replied in a deliberately stilted voice. "Don't all lovers exchange gifts?" She shrugged, too hurt to notice the tightening around his mouth, the clenched muscles in his face. "I mean, you gave me the necklace before the seduction. I just gave you one afterward."

"Francyne, stop this," Brendan commanded quietly, trying to control his anger. "You're making it sound cheap and sordid."

"I didn't mean to," she replied with caustic sweetness. "I only meant to put it in proper perspective." Her voice was cool and quiet. She wiped the tears from her cheeks and she drew up to her full height. She smiled. "You see, I hadn't gone the full route before, and I didn't understand the role of mistress." Her emphasis on the last word left Brendan in no doubt as to her opinion of mistresses in general and of him in particular.

He started to say something, but Francyne shook her head. "Let me finish first," she enjoined in that deathly quiet voice. "You see"—she laughed bitterly, the sound evoking a haunting sadness—"I thought you gave me the necklace because you loved me."

She could see the stunned expression as it crept over Brendan's face, slowly transforming all his features. She could tell that the thought of love had never passed through his conscious mind. He didn't even begin to understand what she was talking about.

Again he started to say something. This time, however, he opened his mouth, but no words came. He didn't know what to say. Never had he encountered a scene like this one. Never had he encountered a woman like this.

"Why did you give me the necklace?" Francyne asked.

Again Brendan looked surprised. "I gave it to you because it was your birthday, and I wanted to give you a gift," he said, still trying to put the pieces of the puzzle together.

"That's not what I mean," she returned softly. "I want to know why you gave me this particular piece of jewelry. Why not something else? Why this chain?"

"Don't you like it?" he asked, stalling for time, wondering what would happen next.

"That's not the point under consideration," she countered. "Why did you buy me this particular chain?"

He shrugged. "Because you liked it, or at least I thought you liked it. You spent enough time admiring it."

Francyne stared at him blankly for a second. Was he lying? Hadn't he been standing there when the saleswoman explained about the necklace? Didn't he understand that it was part of a bridal collection?

"You—" She licked her lips, swallowed, and cleared her throat. "You didn't hear the saleswoman when she said this was part of a bridal collection?" She saw him shake his head and furrow his brows as if he were trying to remember. "She said . . . she said that many couples were buying these today along with the traditional engagement ring because both the man and the woman

. . ." He was still shaking his head. Her voice died to a whisper. " . . . both the man and the woman could wear them."

"Francyne," he breathed, "I swear I didn't know that was what the chain meant. I . . . I . . ." How could he tell her that he was planning her seduction at the same time that the saleswoman was discussing the necklace with her. "I wasn't listening to the saleswoman," he finished inanely. "I was thinking about . . . well . . . about other things at the time."

"You didn't give this to me because you loved me?" she asked, because she had to. She wanted to know.

"No, I didn't give it to you because I loved you," he answered truthfully, because he had to. He owed her that much.

The honesty of his answer didn't relieve her hurt, or her humiliation, or her anger. Her eyes were luminous; they were large; they mirrored all the anguish of her soul. He saw this, and he took a step toward her. He wanted to console her, to explain his feelings for her.

"Don't!" The command was issued in such a soft voice that Brendan wasn't sure he heard it. He took another step. "Don't!" she repeated, a little louder this time. "Don't ever touch me again." She backed away from him, bumping into the dresser. "I understand it all now." She laughed, near-hysteria in her voice. "Imagine how stupid I've been. I guess you've really been laughing at me. I guess I've been rather funny."

"Francyne," Brendan pleaded, for the first time feeling someone else's pain, sharing her anguish, "please, sit down and let's talk. Things aren't totally black or white."

She shook her head, her hair flying around her face. "No," she replied, suddenly realizing there were no tears in her eyes. They burned, and they ached, but they

174

hadn't felt the solace of tears. Her eyes were dry and gritty, as if someone had thrown sand into them. "Quite truthfully," she replied, "I don't think I could listen to any explanations at the moment." She nodded. "I'm sure you're right. It's not all black or white, but . . ." She moved her shoulders slightly. "I don't want to discuss it now."

"Francyne," Brendan pleaded, "we've got something special going. Let's not ruin it."

Francyne smiled sadly. "*Special* has a different meaning for you than it has for me." He shook his head, but Francyne kept on talking. "I'm not ready for your kind of affair, and that's all you're interested in, isn't it? An affair." Still she didn't pause. "I suppose I could go along with that if you loved me, but I refuse to get involved in any kind of relationship based on nothing more than lust."

"Perhaps . . ." Brendan began, in an attempt to reason with her, not understanding that at the moment rational thought was not meaningful to Francyne. Her hurt and mortification blocked out everything but her chagrin. Her calm composure had fooled him. "Perhaps in the beginning I was only thinking about getting you into bed, and the necklace was part of that—"

"Well, congratulations are in order, Mr. O'Shea," Francyne broke in. "You've succeeded. You got me into bed. Now"—she tried to unclasp the necklace, and when she couldn't, she caught the lover's knot in her fist and gave one hard yank. She threw it across the room, watching as it hit him on the chest, then fell to the floor—"you can have your necklace back. Give it to your next partner."

Brendan stooped over and picked up the chain, fingering the broken clasp. He moved across the room, clutching both her shoulders in his hands. "Please listen," he asked. "Let's talk it out. Please."

She looked into his face, her eyes blank, registering nothing.

"Francyne." He guided her over to the bed, sitting her down, sitting down beside her. "When I gave you the necklace I was only thinking about taking you to bed. But I promise you, I bought the necklace because I knew it was something special to you." His brown eyes anxiously searched hers. "I don't speak the same language as you do," he continued. "I don't believe in love, as you see it. If I did—" He searched for the words; he struggled to say them. "If I did—" He didn't know how to complete his sentence honestly.

Francyne stared at him, but she gave him no help. She said nothing; she felt nothing.

"Would it mean anything to you," he finally asked, "if I said I felt differently about you?"

Francyne arched her eyebrows and said, "I feel *differently* about a lot of things, but that doesn't have anything to do with loving. What you're saying doesn't mean much."

"Believe me," Brendan implored, with all the charm he could muster, "we could have a beautiful relationship, one we would both enjoy."

The rich, mellow voice, designed to carry her off with him, went on and on, persuasively gentle and sweet. She heard only the sounds, but she didn't listen to the words. She retreated to a world of numbness. Only this offered her a dignified exit. The numbness guaranteed that she wouldn't make an even bigger fool of herself. No more tears, she knew. No more apologies, she decided.

"And we'll be happy," he concluded, gazing into her face, hoping that he'd convinced her.

"For how long?" she asked curiously.

"As long as it lasts," he replied.

"Without love it can't last too long," she shot back. "And without love I can't be a part of it." She stood up, escaping from the closeness of his body, moving over to the window. "I told you that I want more from a man than sex." She smiled at Brendan. "Just think, you asked me not to marry Sterling because all he could offer me was sex. Now look at what you're offering me."

The argument had lasted longer, but she remained adamant in her refusal to live with him on his terms. When he had exhausted all points of persuasion and had lapsed into silence, she had asked him to drive her to the airport. She wanted to come home. At first he had refused outright, but when she obstinately insisted, he finally relented. He promised to drive her to the airport, on condition that she cool off and talk things over with him when he returned to San Antonio. Quietly, as she packed her cases, she listened as he outlined his plans. As she had suspected, he took her silence for affirmation.

Now he was back and ready to resume their—what? Friendship? Surely not that. Their affair? Hardly that! Their relationship? Perhaps! He fully expected her to change her mind, she thought. That's how self-assured and confident he is! And if she gave in to the way she felt about him, she would accept him on any terms. She loved him, and she wanted him. She wanted to be with him all the time.

She forced herself to stay where she was, and she betrayed none of her inner turmoil. Slowly she turned to face him, and she watched as he drained the last drop of liquor from his glass. She watched as he stood and walked to the bar to fix himself a second drink. She saw the movements of his arms; she heard the clink of the cubes against the side of the glass; she heard the splash of the scotch. Then he retraced his steps and ensconced himself in the chair again.

Brendan quirked his brow and scowled in her direction, his eyes flitting over her dress. "I don't like that thing"—he didn't know the word for it—"that dress that you're wearing."

"It doesn't matter if you do or not," Francyne returned, smiling inwardly, "I didn't pick it out with you in mind."

"Would you go put something on that fits you?"

"I don't want to," she replied steadily, her smile growing into a small chuckle.

"Well, then," he snapped, disconcerted, "will you sit down?"

"I don't want to," she replied in the same even tone, her lips finally twitching.

"I want you to!" he thundered, giving in to frustration and anger.

He downed his drink in several large gulps and set the glass on the coffee table with a heavy thud. He ran his fingers around the collar and unbuttoned another button. Still it wasn't enough so that Francyne could see the gold chain. Which one was he wearing?

Brendan had never been so angry at a woman in his entire life. When Francyne had left him last Sunday, he'd been dumbfounded. At first he had thought he was upset because his plans had gone awry, but later as he sat around and brooded about it, he realized that he was more angry at himself for having let her go. He discovered as soon as she was gone that he cared for her.

He had caught the next plane out, arriving in San Antonio just a few hours after her. And much to his surprise Francyne wasn't home when he arrived. During the past week he had called many times; he'd come over many times. He had haunted the travel agency, but no one knew where she was. He had even driven out to the lake house, but he found only her parents, and if they knew where she was, they didn't tell him.

He didn't want to go through another week like the past one. He'd almost gone crazy wondering where she was, wondering who she was with. His eyes darted back to the chain that was hanging around her neck. That irritated him beyond measure.

"Where did you get that chain?" he rasped, the words out before he knew that he'd said them.

"A friend."

Before Francyne knew what had happened, he was standing in front of her, his hands gripping her shoulders, glaring into her face. She could see the anger that contorted his features, the tension in his face, the white tightness around his mouth. When one hand left her shoulder and the fingers curled around the chain, Francyne spoke.

"Don't take it off."

How did she know that he was going to take it off? He dropped his hand.

Too quietly he said, "Then you take it off."

She stared at him, the adrenaline pumping through her veins, the blood hammering in her temples, her heart beating so fast she could hardly get her breath. She was playing a dangerous game, but it was exhilarating. She hadn't felt this alive since last weekend.

"Perhaps I don't want to take it off. Perhaps it means something to me."

"Francyne." He spoke her name softly. "Turn around and let me take off this chain."

Dear God, he thought, what am I coming to? Since

when has a trinket like this become such a paramount issue? Why do I feel that I've got to strip her of everything that isn't mine? Why am I jealous of this insignificant trifle?

Francyne wished she could read his mind, because she wasn't sure of his motivation at the moment. She would have loved to know what he was thinking. She hoped that he'd been as miserable as she had. She hoped that he'd come to love her as she loved him.

"Why do you want me to take it off?"

He looked at her for what seemed like forever before he reached into his pocket and held up another chain. "I want you to wear this one."

Francyne gaped at the delicate strand of gold that dangled precariously from one of his fingers. "You bought me another chain just like the first one," she said quietly. She raised her stunned face, her eyes flitting from the chain to his. "That was rather silly." She swallowed her tears. "Why did you do it?"

"I know what it means to you," he said finally. "This time I want to put it on you, knowing what it means to you."

Francyne was breathing rapidly now, and her breasts were rising and falling with every breath. Brendan's eyes took in every inch of her. When he raised his eyes and Francyne saw the undisguised hunger that raged in them, she felt her breasts swell and tighten; she felt her nipples harden. Brendan's eyes moved down again, looking first at the white gold chain, then lower at the crested buds that were discernible through the cotton fabric.

His hand, loosely folded into a fist, brushed against her breasts, the knuckles in his hand teasing them with their touch. Up and down he lightly moved the hand—almost touching, touching, not touching. The throbbing in her body, the ache in her stomach and her breasts, the emptiness within her, reacted to the silent invitation. She leaned forward, pressing herself against him.

But she couldn't give in yet. "I know what it means to me," she whispered, "but I want to know what it means to you."

His hand stopped moving, resting against her breast. "I'm willing to give it a try," he agreed with a sigh. "If it works, fine, if it doesn't . . ." He shrugged, letting Francyne guess at the rest of his thought.

"You're willing to give what a try?" she asked, that familiar pain clutching at her heart.

"You want marriage," he said. "I'm willing to try it."

She shook her head. "You still don't understand," she said sadly.

He unbuttoned his shirt and pulled it open. "Look," he said, "I'm wearing your chain, and I know what it means to you. I'm willing to try marriage! What more do you want?"

"I only want your love," she replied faintly. "I want it to be given freely, not like this. I want you to be sure that you love me too."

She lifted a hand and touched his face, letting her fingers gently massage the faint stubble on his cheeks. "I know that I love you," she said, "and I know that I want to marry you." Her eyes smiled into his. "But I'm not ready to go into marriage with the idea that it's not going to work."

"Are you telling me no?" he asked flatly, his brown eyes dull with an inexpressible pain.

"Yes." She nodded. "I'm telling you no."

He held the chain out. "Will you take the chain?" She shook her head. "No!"

She didn't want the chain. She wanted him, all of him. She wanted to take him under any circumstances, but she knew it wouldn't work. She wasn't prepared for a one-sided love affair or a halfhearted attempt at marriage.

"Will I see you again?" The same question he'd asked the first time he'd met her.

Tears welled up in her eyes, and she shook her head. "No." Her voice was tremulous. "Under the circumstances it would be best for us—"

He raised a brow questioningly. "Us?"

"For me," she corrected herself. "Not to see you again."

"Why?"

Even the question was sensuous; it seduced her senses, her reasoning. He exerted all his persuasive charm. He couldn't walk off and leave her. He didn't know if he loved her or not, but, dear God, he knew he wanted her. He wanted her with every fiber of his being.

"You know why," she replied, the sorceress's eyes gently chiding him. "I wouldn't be able to refuse you."

"Would that be so bad?" he asked, a whimsical smile curving his lips.

"For me it would be so bad," she whispered, her decision releasing a second flood of anguish and heart-break.

"Okay," he said, determined to hide his pain from her, disguising it with flippancy. Carelessly he dropped the chain into his pocket. "If that's the way you want it."

"It's not the way I want it," she replied softly, "but it's the only way it can be for me. It's the only way I can salvage myself and my feelings."

He nodded, walked to the sofa, and picked up his jacket, slinging it over his shoulder rather than putting it on. He moved to the door, closed his hand over the knob, and twisted it but didn't pull the door open.

"Any chance of your changing your mind?"

"Not until you change yours," she answered, turning her back, unable to watch him walk out of her life.

Then she heard the soft good-bye, then the thud of the door as it closed behind him; then she was alone, all alone. Transfixed, she stood at the window, staring into the courtyard, wondering why she'd let Brendan walk away from her. She knew that her life wouldn't be complete without him, and she knew that he had come as near to proclaiming his love for her as he could. Knowing that, she castigated herself for not being more understanding, for acting so impulsively.

How long had she been standing there? She didn't know. What did it matter? She spun on her heels and ran to the door, fumbling with the lock, unable to grasp the knob and pull on the door at the same time. She had to catch him. She couldn't lose him. They'd work their differences out. They would!

She sped across the small front terrace and out the gate, opening her mouth to shout after him, when she bumped into a solid wall of flesh. Two arms closed around her in the tightest vise she'd ever felt. Startled, she looked up into Brendan's face, hers a mirror of anxiety and despair.

Brendan looked down, his arms around her, his hands splaying across her back. Gently he smiled, his eyes frolicking with happiness. He didn't say a word; he just held her, burying his face in that satiny-sweet curve of her shoulder.

Trying to muster up some indignation, Francyne sputtered, "You weren't leaving at all! You just wanted me to come running after you!"

But she couldn't keep her lips from curving into a

glorious smile; she couldn't keep her soul from singing as her heart played the melody of love and the blood danced through her veins.

"No," he agreed, "I couldn't walk away and leave you." His smile deepened; both were drinking from the same well of emotion. "I tried, but I didn't get any farther than the car. I was coming back because you're very special to me."

Francyne chuckled, her voice muffled against his chest. "I wasn't going to let you go either." She raised her face, her eyes a vibrant blue. "I couldn't let you go because I love you."

The brown eyes solemnly gazed into the so-sure eyes below. He wished love could come that easily to him. For her sake he wished he could love as unconditionally as she.

"Go get out of this bag," he said, one hand balling into a fist, gripping a wad of the loose material of her dress. "And let's go out to eat. Then we'll talk. Okay?"

Not the answer she'd quite hoped for, but she wouldn't let her disappointment cloud the radiant happiness that was shining in her eyes. She and Brendan would work out their differences. They would!

CHAPTER EIGHT

The bridegroom in his navy Devon stood on the stage of the Arneson River Theater in front of Pastor Kenneth Jamison. His eyes, however, were focused on the woman who was standing at the top of the steps of the amphitheater across the river. He didn't see Keeley or Sophia as they walked down the stairs ahead of the bride, nor did he see John LaRue, who was escorting his younger daughter.

Brendan was aware of no one but his bride as she descended the steps in the early-evening sunlight. Her white satin and lace gown recalled the Victorian era with its gathered sleeves and its long A-line skirt and semi-cathederal train. Completing her bridal regalia was the headpiece, a lace broad-brimmed hat with its flowing veil. As she stepped across the stone bridge that spanned the river, separating her from the theater seats, setting her on the stage, bringing her closer to her bridegroom, her eyes caught and held those of the man whom she loved and was about to marry.

When her soft, red lips parted into a smile, Brendan's

face glowed with rapturous awe. The soft rays of the evening sun surrounded her with an unearthly glow, and he wondered if she was human or if perhaps she was a river enchantress! But he didn't care as long as she belonged to him. He was ensnared in her magic web, and he silently implored her never to free him from her love.

His lips curved into an answering smile, and he held out his hand, waiting for her to join him. He didn't want her suddenly to disappear; he didn't want to lose her before she really became his. He would have laughed anyone to shame a few weeks ago if they had suggested that he would love someone as much as he loved Francyne, that he would love a woman enough to marry her. But now . . . He smiled from his soul, his eyes and his mouth reflecting the beautiful tenderness of his feelings.

He was marrying her because he loved her and because he wanted to marry her. He hadn't minded all the sentimentality that was connected with the ritual. The family minister! The after-six look! The river wedding!

But he had insisted on the traditional ceremony with only a few minor changes.

"Do you take this woman . . ."

Yes, I take this woman for life. Nothing short of that will satisfy me.

"To love, to honor, to cherish . . ."

I love her, I honor her, I cherish her.

"With this ring I thee wed. . . ."

The brown eyes, made solemn by the intensity of Brendan's love, gazed into the wide hazel eyes that were shaded by the lace-brimmed hat. He held the ring loosely between his thumb and fingers. This was his surprise. Together they had chosen the engagement ring, but he had asked Francyne to let him surprise her with the wedding ring. He wanted to choose that himself.

He took her left hand in his, and with his right hand he held up a small yellow gold band for her to see. Before he slipped it on her finger, he spoke, and the words were love-soft, meant only for her ears.

"Look, my darling . . ." He held the ring up so that she could see it. "It's a gold lover's knot that binds you to my side."

Not caring that this wasn't part of the written ceremony or that people were watching, Francyne took the ring and looked at the intricate work of art. "It's beautiful," she told him, tears glimmering in her eyes. Her voice softened to a whispered sigh. "But it's not the knot that ties me to your side. It's my love for you."

"Do you mind?" he asked, taking the ring from her unresisting fingers.

She shook her head. "I don't. Do you?"

"I wouldn't settle for less. I had that once, and I was miserable. Now I want more."

He slid the ring onto her finger.

"I had the ring designed so that the knot ties on top, symbolically binding you and me together." He peered into her soul. "Because it is circular, there is no beginning or ending to our happiness." His thumb stroked around the center of the ring. "The diamond that rests in the center is symbolic of the solidity of our love and our marriage."

Two small teardrops appeared on her cheeks, washing away the question that had marred the beauty of her eyes.

"I love you, my wife."

"For how long?" she whispered.

"Forever."

She moved closer to him, and her lips lightly touched

his cheek. But he felt as if her flesh had burned a brand onto his cheek. He raised his hand, his fingers touching the spot where her lips had rested. He knew that it wouldn't matter if he wore the gold chain or not, or whether he wore the wedding band or not. He would always carry the mark of her love. He would never be the same again.

When You Want A Little More Than Romance—

Try A Candlelight Ecstasy!

Jacqueline Briskin

author of Paloverde and The Onyx

Rich Friends

Beautiful, talented, wealthy and powerful, they thought the California skies held no limits. And life is so much more exciting when you have rich friends!

"Two generations of a wealthy Southern California family and the effect that family has on those whose lives they touch. To this format, Miss Briskin brings a serious tone and a degree of skill all too rare in these generational epics." —*The Los Angeles Times*

"Good storytelling, suspense, and a wow of an ending. You'll go for this book."
—*The San Francisco Chronicle*

A DELL BOOK   17380-9 $3.95